JURY OF ONE

by Mignon G. Eberhart

Equation for murder. Let A equal a triangle of suspicion, jealousy and hatred; let B equal a tangled family situation, with love and money at stake; let C equal control of the Beall-Esk Company machine works, presently undergoing financial reorganization. A + B + C equal X, the unknown murderer.

Growing up in a New England town, Kirk Beall, Maggy, and Josh, son of the local doctor, were friends, as were their families. Then came the war. Things changed, and Kirk, a dashing young go-getter, took his position as head of the family company to revitalize its lagging business. After a whirlwind courtship, he and Maggy were to be married—the ideal union. Then, three days before the wedding, Josh, now with a New York brokerage firm, turned up unexpectedly and confronted Maggy in the rose arbor. "You can't marry Kirk," he said. "He's not the man for you."

There were other fateful meetings in the rose arbor and in a canoe on the swift-flowing river. There was an accident and a drowning, and another death under mysterious circumstances. Was either fatality murder? Yes, said Josh. Was Maggy implicated? What were her chances of survival amidst the strange actions of people she thought she knew so well? What did Josh mean when he said to Maggy, "You could scream all you like and no one would hear you?"

Mrs. Eberhart spins a fascinating web of loyalties and hatred, with the business reorganization lurking like an evil being in the background.

JURY OF ONE

JURY
OF
ONE

MIGNON G. EBERHART

RANDOM HOUSE *New York*

FIRST PRINTING

© Copyright, 1960, by Mignon G. Eberhart

All rights reserved under International and Pan-American Copyright
Conventions. Published in New York by Random House, Inc., and
simultaneously in Toronto, Canada, by Random House of Canada,
Limited.

LIBRARY OF CONGRESS CATALOG CARD NUMBER: 60-5543
Manufactured in the United States of America
by the Colonial Press Inc.

JURY OF ONE

ONE

Late in the afternoon Maggy escaped the house and found the old path that twisted through woods and shrubbery upward to the lookout point above the river. The murmur of the river grew more distinct as the path wound closer to it. A rose bramble snaked out to catch at her ankle as she emerged from the path and stood on the little rocky promontory high above the house and the river.

There were too many roses, she thought; there were great clusters of them everywhere, blood red in the summer sun.

The view was the same and yet not the same.

There was of course the great loop of the Matoax as it came full spate from the dam at Milbridge twenty miles to the north and sped between rocky woodlands on the Milrock side and broad pastures and distant hills on the opposite side. The river then curved and disappeared beyond the woods south of the house. The rocks, which just there declined sharply from the promontory to the river, were massed with honeysuckle and ramblers. The blue hills far across the river and beyond the rich green farmlands were veiled with a purplish heat haze. The sun made golden, dappled patterns on the river.

She remembered the view as one remembers a picture seen long ago; it was the same picture, yet subtly different, as if fancy had added some color which was not there in fact.

Her childhood fancy had supplied the river not with Indians, or British redcoats, or Dutch explorers which its name, the Matoax, might have conjured up, but with boats which had sails of gold; the pastures and far-off hills with castles. Perhaps she had then been reading of King Arthur, she thought, amused.

Down at the house they were still taking gifts from their wrappings; the big room was strewn with excelsior and white tissue paper. On Friday, after the wedding on Thursday, the array of silver and crystal and china would have to be sorted out and places found for all of it. She looked down toward the house but the woods seemed to have changed, too; the trees were taller and thicker and curtained with wild grapevines. She could barely see a chimney or two, masked with ivy.

She wiped her arm across her moist forehead. The sun was full and hot on her face. Behind her the old rose arbor still stood, a trellised enclosure on three sides with the fourth side open upon the view of the river. The roof sagged as if from the weight of the roses but it offered a little shade. She went in, tested one of the rustic chairs and sat down gingerly; it was solid though, made of redwood to last forever like the solid bricks of the house. She looked out over the river, through the golden sunlight.

She wished vaguely that she had brought cigarettes and searched the pockets of her tailored blue linen shorts and white shirt but found no crumpled package, not even a bent cigarette. It wasn't worth going back to the house through the brambles and the honeysuckle and heat to get a cigarette. Besides she would be caught again with some

4

question about the wedding preparations which had to be decided then and there.

Her eyes half closed against the light, she sank into a dreamy reverie. If boats with golden sails no longer skimmed along the river, if castles no longer reared themselves in romance upon the far-off hills, still a fairy story colored the whole of it, her own fairy story. Her marriage was to bring her back to live in this place, this house. She was Cinderella.

She smiled, deprecating her own extravagance. She, Maggy Warren, a sensible twenty-two, a registered nurse who had earned her own bread and butter for several years, and whose eyes had to be more or less open to the ways of the world, would be no fairy princess, even though she was to marry the prince.

As clearly as the view before her now, she could see the little town of Milrock, two miles away, and the white clapboard cottage on Elm Street where she had grown up. The cottage had been intended merely as a temporary refuge, where she and her mother, Cornelia Warren, could wait for the war to end and Maggy's father to return from service in the Navy. He did not return and the temporary refuge became a permanent home for Maggy and her mother. Of all the cogent arguments for remaining in Milrock one of the strongest was Cornelia Warren's close friendship with Emily Beall.

Perhaps every small town has its big house presided over by its leading, elegant but slightly removed and awe-inspiring family. In Milrock it was the Beall family and the Beall house. The Beall house did not change; it was built to last. The Beall family had undergone the inevitable changes of the years. The Bealls of Maggy's generation were Kirk and Clare, brother and sister. Kirk was older than Clare; Clare was older than Maggy. During her childhood the gap of years between Clare and Maggy was too much for companionship, certainly too much for a sharing of any childish interests. Clare was almost a young lady, Kirk was a young man, while Maggy was still a child; so Maggy could only worship from afar these glittering beings who lived in what seemed to her an enchanted and luxurious castle. Even as Maggy grew up and the gap of years gradually closed between the three of them, Clare remained remote; she never really knew Clare. Besides, Clare was always away at school and when she was at home she was at the piano. But Cousin Emily was from the first like a dear and elderly aunt to Maggy.

Indeed she took the place of aunt—and mother and father—to Clare and Kirk and had done so almost all their lives. During Maggy's childhood she had taken Cousin Emily for granted; she was always there, seeing to the house, seeing to Kirk and Clare. Sometime, though, Maggy discovered that Cousin Emily Beall was exactly that—a cousin of Clare and Kirk's father who had come to the Beall house first when Clare and Kirk's mother died, to keep house and take care of her cousin's children, and she had naturally taken over when, several years later, Kirk and Clare's father died.

Emily Beall was older than Maggy's mother but from the first there had existed between them the kind of mutual understanding which goes beyond definition and establishes an immediate kinship. When the young Navy wife became a widow Emily Beall became a tower of strength and friendliness.

There were others, of course, who made Cornelia Warren feel that Milrock was her home. Dr. Mason and his son, Josh, who lived in the house next door were towers of strength and support, too—Dr. Mason because that was his nature and Josh because Cornelia's generous motherliness had extended itself to Josh, who had no mother. Josh loved Cornelia and in a reticent, New England way tried as a boy might to look after Cornelia and consequently Maggy.

Indeed at her last meeting with Josh—well, that hadn't meant anything, she thought swiftly and with, even now, a touch of amused surprise. In any event Josh had gone off to his military service, she had returned to Milrock after her graduation from nurses' training school, and her mother had gone to Paris.

Cornelia Warren's job in Paris sounded glamorous. Maggy suspected that it was not, but it was, as her mother explained, a job and it had offered itself at the right time. An old school friend, a fashion writer, had needed an assistant, a leg woman, she told Cornelia Warren; Maggy was by then away from home; why should Cornelia, still a young woman, stagnate in Milrock with nothing to do? Cornelia had rather objected to the word *stagnate* but, since Maggy was no longer at home, she did want a job of some kind and the income from it, though small, was not unwelcome. She hesitated about putting the Atlantic Ocean between herself and Maggy but Maggy, mature enough to see Cornelia as a woman needing to lead her own life, as well as a mother, overcame Cornelia's doubts. The white cottage was sold. Someone else now pruned the great lilacs and struggled with the balky chimney flue. But the Beall house remained just as it had been during the days when Maggy's visits there were hours of enchantment. In those days, too, Kirk had been as glittering and far away as the stars.

No matter how sensibly she looked at it, her marriage

7

was still as romantic as anything her childhood fancy had evoked.

A twig snapped in the woods that stretched up and over the hillside, which backed the arbor and the lookout point. There was a crash of footsteps and the rustle of undergrowth. Whoever was coming through the woods came in a rush, as if sliding on the carpet of pine needles, grasped at the arbor so the whole structure shook and seemed to encounter a rose bramble, for he said, "*Ouch!*" Then he came around the arbor and stood outlined against the low, western sun, at the very edge of the rocks, looking across the broad Matoax and sucking his wrist.

He wore khaki-colored slacks and shirt, which had been washed so often that they were nearly white. His figure blocked itself out, tall and sturdy against the light. His sandy hair was cut short and thick. There was a compactness as of springy hard muscles about him. Maggy cried, "Josh!"

He turned around quickly, his hazel eyes bright with recognition and astonishment. "Maggy! What are *you* doing here?"

She met him at the door of the arbor. She didn't remember that Josh was so much taller and bigger than she was; his arms went around her and lifted her up a little to meet his light kiss on her cheek. He drew back, still holding her while he looked down into her eyes. It was a long look, half laughing, growing more serious, and suddenly deeply lighted. He drew her close to him again and kissed her mouth.

The sun enfolded them in its golden warmth. The river rippled and purled, concealing its latent strength and seeming very far away. Everything seemed far away except the pressure of Josh's lips upon her own and the warmth of his arms. And then Maggy thought, this is what happened the last time we met.

That time it had been at the little railway station in Milrock—at night, with the crickets and tree frogs chirping away and the light at the station door haloed with fog.

Surprise caught her, as it had then, but this time dismay caught her, too. She drew away from him abruptly but Josh let her go as abruptly.

He was surprised, too, she thought. Josh never seemed abashed or taken aback but he was surprised. He passed one hand over sandy hair and looked at her now with a gleam of laughter in his hazel eyes. He remembered, too. "Last time you kissed me was when I left to go to camp."

"You kissed me, you mean!"

His eyes narrowed. "Oh, you kissed back. Although come to think of it, that was the first time. That is—like that . . ."

He was suddenly watching her rather closely. He was teasing; she knew that bright gleam away back in his eyes.

All the same she wished she hadn't been caught off balance, like that, by surprise. It was sheer man-woman magnetism but it was sheer nonsense, too.

She said shortly, "You're not the only man I've ever kissed. . . . It's cooler in the arbor." She went back to the rustic chair.

Josh followed as far as the entrance where he stood, framed by the roses and the sunlight, his back to the river. "Tell me about the others," he said lazily, the bright, teasing gleam still in his eyes. "I want to hear all about them."

"Well, you're not going to. When did you get back?"

"Last night." He put his hand on a corner post and shook it. The arbor and the roses shook, too, and some red petals

9

drifted down. "I expected that this place had crumbled and fallen into the river by now."

"Then you've seen your father?"

"As a matter of fact I haven't. I got out of the Army last week, came to New York and . . ." he paused briefly, then said rather tersely, "got my old job back. Came up here late last night. My father was out on a late call and was gone to the office by the time I got up this morning. We've talked over the phone but that's all." He came into the arbor, tested a chair and lowered himself into it cautiously. It creaked but held and he drew a package of cigarettes from his pocket, offered it to her and held a lighter for her.

Above the little flame she took a quick look at his face, so near her own. It was older, a little firmer around the wide mouth and straight, New England nose, a little tighter around the hard jawline. His sandy eyebrows were sunbleached and stood out whitely against his tanned skin. He was aware of her scrutiny and looked up, his gray-green eyes twinkling. "You'll know me next time."

"I knew you the instant I saw you."

"Well—I knew you." But he gave her a long, measuring look and said, "You've changed."

An age-old feminine instinct nudged her. "Have I changed?"

Immediately she wished she hadn't said it for one of Josh's sandy eyebrows quirked up. "Fishing for compliments?"

"No!" Josh could always prick any little balloon of vanity she tentatively launched.

When she was a little girl and Josh a big boy he had indulged her and looked after her. During her self-important teens, however, he had given her the brusque and

10

deflating treatment of an elder brother whenever he felt she needed it—until the night he went into the Army.

So after three years she had gone straight into his arms again! This will never do, she told herself, and Josh said unexpectedly, "You were a long-legged, tanned, nice little girl. You were an exasperating teen-ager—pretty and you knew it. When I last saw you, you were—how old, twenty?—and beautiful and you didn't know it. Now you're a woman and . . ." he paused and then said dryly, "You'll do. But don't let it go to your head."

She laughed. "I'm not likely to. You haven't changed one bit, Josh."

"Nothing has changed." He looked around him thoughtfully.

Probably for him, too, the shabby little arbor, the long view of the river, were packed with memories—herself, Josh, Kirk and Clare.

Kirk, of course, in those days was a dazzling and far-off figure to Maggy—a young man in college when she and Josh were still children, later starting his spectacular career of building up the Beall-Esk Company at a time when Josh was playing football and Maggy was in grade school.

There had been a vast age barrier between them all, once. It was when Maggy was about seventeen that the age barrier began to slide away. Kirk was still as remote and glittering as the stars but Josh, home week ends from the university and then from his job in New York, had occasionally taken her dancing. Clare had married a Southerner named Alroy Fisher and disappeared from the Beall house for a time. Maggy had entered nurses' training school in Boston. Josh had left for his military service. Up to now she had hardly known him.

Now that they were all adults there was no age barrier

at all. Josh said suddenly and rather soberly, "I was thinking about Kirk. When I was in college, I was going to be like him—dashing around in fast sports cars, taking over a failing company and putting it on its feet. So I turned into a broker and then a G.I. and now an ex-G.I." He broke off. "What are your eyes so big about?"

"Josh, you haven't heard! Didn't your father tell you —well, of course, he couldn't have, but oh, Josh, you've got to stay till Thursday. You've got to come to the wedding."

Josh's face was completely still. "Whose wedding?"

"Why, my wedding! To Kirk. On Thursday. At the church. Here in Milrock."

He gave her a long, straight look. Then he rose and went to stand in the entrance, leaning one shoulder against the corner post. "So that's why you're here. I thought you were visiting Miss Emily or . . . Tell me about all this. When did it happen?"

"Why—well, really just all at once. I mean, this spring."

"I see. A whirlwind courtship?"

"Not at all! I've known Kirk all my life! Don't tease, Josh."

"I'm not teasing. Go on. Tell me about it."

She eyed his broad shoulders and sandy head doubtfully. It was hard to tell just what Josh was thinking but he didn't seem to be in the mood for tender confidences. On the other hand, when they were younger he had always been quick to defend her and to sympathize when sympathy was needed. A swift mental picture presented itself to her: Josh soberly burying her loved old yellow cat who had engaged in one battle too many and then taking her to the corner drug store for a restoring ice cream soda. And later, as soberly, taking her part when she determined

12

to go into nurses' training and her mother had objected. "She's got to go to college," her mother had said, worry over the money that four years of college would require sharpening her usually warm voice. But Josh had seen both sides of it. "Let her go," he said and put his arms around Cornelia. "She wants to try her wings."

Maggy wanted to learn a profession as cheaply and as quickly as she could; she'd wanted to earn her way. Josh had known that.

She said, "I came up here, to Milrock, this spring to see about some books Mother had stored here. Miss Emily invited me to stay over the week end. Kirk was here and—it was the first time really we'd seen each other—I mean, I'm grown up now and—well, that's the way it happened."

"A romance."

"Yes!" There was the faintest edge of defiance in her voice and she heard it. "It really is a romance, Josh. We're going to be married on Thursday. Then we'll take the night plane to Paris."

There was a rather long silence. Then Josh threw away his cigarette and turned to her. "I'm sorry, Maggy. It won't do. You can't marry Kirk."

He really sounded as if he meant it. "But—why, that's —I'm twenty-two! I'm quite capable of . . ."

"And Kirk, if I'm right, is about thirty-seven."

"Suppose he is! What difference does that make?"

"Look out." Josh reached a swift hand to flick away a burning ash which had fallen from her cigarette onto her blue shorts. Her own hand went automatically to brush at the ash, too, and met his and she jerked her hand away as if there were some reason why she must not touch his hand even for so brief an instant.

Josh perceived the gesture and the reason for it; he gave

13

a little chuckle. She rose. "I've got to go back to the house. I've got lots to do and . . ."

"If you've got so much to do, why are you sitting around here? Looking at the roses?"

"Never mind what I was doing. Now I am going back and . . ." She took a quick breath. "Oh, Josh, let's not talk like this! I am glad you're home. I'm glad to see you again. And I do so much want you to come to the wedding. . . ."

"I told you. You can't marry Kirk."

"But Josh—oh, don't talk like that! Why on earth not?"

"Because Kirk is not the man for you." Again, and incredibly, he sounded as if he meant it.

Yet he wasn't serious; he couldn't be serious.

He walked out to the ledge of rocks and looked down. After a moment he said over his shoulder in a curiously absent way, almost as if talking to himself, "You could scream here until you were blue in the face and nothing but the roses would hear you."

TWO

It was an isolated place, the little lookout point so high above the river, so remote from the house, so closely surrounded by woods and curtains of wild grapevines and roses. The house itself was isolated in a way with swampy woodlands to the south, the river to the west, rocky woodlands to the north and its grounds sloping eastward, down through woods and shrubbery again, to the public highway.

But there was nothing to scream about, Maggy thought suddenly. Nothing at all. Kirk shouted from the path lower down, "Maggy—are you up there?"

She turned toward the path as Kirk came around the curve of pine trees and laurels. "They want you at the house. . . . Why, Josh Mason!" Kirk's smile was always one of great charm and friendliness. He put out his hand. "How are you? Are you out of the Army now? When did you get back?"

They shook hands. It seemed to Maggy that Josh's hand broke away rather quickly. He said, "Last night."

"Just in time for the wedding! Maggy's told you?"

"Yes."

"If I'd known you were coming I'd have asked you to be my best man."

"Ah," said Josh.

15

"Well, let's go down to the house. Come on, Josh, we'll have a cold drink."

"Thanks. I just came up through the woods to take a look at the old place. I've got to be getting back. It's a long walk."

Kirk lifted his black eyebrows in an amused way. "You don't mean you walked all the way from Milrock! That's two miles."

"Well," Josh said rather dryly, "I just got out of the Army."

Kirk's light gray eyes ran over Josh's figure. "You look like a fit physical specimen, but I'll take you on at tennis any time. How about tomorrow?"

"All right," Josh said after the barest pause.

"Splendid. Clare and Cousin Emily will want to see you, too. And you remember Alroy Fisher—Clare's husband."

"I remember Alroy."

"Good. I'm afraid the tennis court is not up to much. It's not been used. I have been too busy. But come on anyway."

Josh didn't look at Maggy. And he was different—polite and pleasant enough but remote and impersonal at the same time. The difference was so marked in Maggy's eyes that she felt a little flick of uneasiness. Josh had been teasing her—that or he had got a notion in his stubborn head that Kirk was too old for her, something of the kind. Yet he was different and she didn't know how or exactly why, only that the difference was there.

He said, "Thanks, Kirk. Tomorrow."

Kirk looked up at the tangle of greens behind the arbor. "You must like the woods and brambles—strolling through on such a hot day. I'll have to have all that cleared out. I don't know when I've been up here. The underbrush seems to have gone wild."

"So have the roses," Josh said. "Too many of them."

"What?" Kirk gave him a rather startled look. "Well—perhaps they have."

The blood red clusters surrounded them close, as if to listen. The green foliage was languid and heavy with heat. There was no shadow over the sun; it was only lowering swiftly now toward the distant line of hills. But just for a second it was as if some swift shadow passed over all three of them, standing there together. Then it had passed and had never been. Kirk said, "See you tomorrow, Josh," linked Maggy's arm within his own and they started back down the path.

There was no sound from behind them, no rustle of Josh's departure through the woods. Maggy didn't look back but she was sure that Josh was standing perfectly still, watching until they turned around the bank of pines and laurels and were out of sight.

Kirk held back the brambles for her passage and talked of building a new arbor. "I'll make it a real summerhouse. Glass, I think—just enough steel and concrete to hold it together. Some modern chairs."

She said, "Yes," and thought about Josh with a kind of troubled exasperation. But the thing to do, she decided, was not to think about Josh. Nothing he said or did could possibly affect her or her marriage to Kirk.

Kirk lifted a long loop of roses so she could pass below it as they came out on the level stretch of green lawn, which was now only a few feet above the river. He laughed down into her face and said, "No thorns for you, my darling. Ever."

The path had descended steeply. From the level lawn the view of the river was cut off by the great trees, and the crowding willows that went to its very banks, but there were bright silvery gleams through the lacy willows. From the opposite end of the terrace other steps led to a flagstone path which rounded the house from the front, went down past the tennis court, humpy now from disuse but with its high backstops laden with roses, and on to the small landing which jutted out over the rocky shallows of the river. A canoe floated in the water beside the landing and a rowboat lay upside down on the grass, below the willows. Shadows now were long across the lawn and upon the house which seemed to watch them from windows heavily draped in ivy and wisteria and, always, roses. There were bright chairs on the terrace, which was now cool and shady. A tray with glasses and ice stood on a low glass table

Kirk pulled up a long chair for her, poured some iced tea and put the glass in her hand. He mixed a drink for himself, sat down in a chair near her with a sigh and leaned back. "Good to be home," he said and drank slowly.

His slender, aquiline features were outlined clearly against the greens beyond the terrace. He had already changed from office clothes and his brown slacks were miraculously unwrinkled, his beige sports shirt looked as if it had come from the best tailor at that very instant. His black hair with its unexpected few strands of white, was crisp and damp as if he had just taken a shower. He had startlingly clear, light gray eyes which looked clearer and lighter because of his black eyelashes and black eyebrows. Kirk always looked elegant.

"A real glamour boy," one of the nurses had said and sighed. "Good looks, charm. And money."

"He's a financial genius," Emily Beall had said with pride.

He wasn't that; Kirk had heard Emily and laughed and denied it. "Make allowances for a fond mother," he had said to Maggy. "At least she's the same as a mother; she's given all her life to me and to Clare."

After the wedding Emily was to travel; she was to go to Switzerland and if she liked it buy a house there. Kirk was generous, Maggy knew; he owed much to Emily but he would do far more for her than Emily Beall would ever expect.

He was going to give his sister Clare and her husband Alroy a house of their own, too—in Milbridge, near the Beall works—as he had given Alroy a job in the Company.

She said, "Did you have a good day?"

He was lost in some intent thought of his own; he gave her a quick smile. "Excellent. Lots of details to see to before we leave. I'll have to put in a long day at the office tomorrow. I'd rather stay here. How is everything going?"

"Cousin Emily and Clare have seen to everything. They don't let me do a thing."

"They like it. They're fond of you."

"They've been perfectly wonderful to me! Inviting me to stay here! Doing everything my mother would have done! Seeing to all the wedding plans and the reception—I didn't know there was so much to do!"

He laughed indulgently. "But I told you. They like it and they're delighted about our marriage. Besides, where would you stay if not here? If your mother could have come, Cousin Emily would have wanted her here, too. This is your home."

"Well, but—not yet."

He laughed again. "Darling, you are such a child. Certainly this is your home and everything in it belongs to you. Have you tried your new car?"

"Oh! No." She felt herself blushing a little. The week before Kirk had brought home a long luxurious car which was to be for her use only. After being admired by the whole family it was now standing in the peaked-roof garage.

"Why not?"

"Why, I—just thought I'd wait." It was not possible to explain that the car didn't seem to belong to her but belonged instead to somebody who didn't really exist, somebody in a magic world who wouldn't even be Maggy.

He said, dreamily, looking out across the lawn, "When our plans for the works mature, you can have as many cars as you want."

She laughed. "One is enough. How are things going?"

"Very well. As soon as we get the stock on the market we're going to branch out—all kinds of ways. The sky is the limit."

She knew something of the works. Everybody in the vicinity and many outside, now that Kirk was in control, knew of the Beall Company.

The factory had been started by Kirk's grandfather, Eleazar Beall, on a shoestring, with a partner (Ludwig Esk), manufacturing small tools in a small way. The original old brick building still stood on the banks of the river in Milbridge.

Eleazar Beall had built it into a substantial and respected business and bought out his partner; it was still, however, a relatively small concern, owned entirely by the Beall family. It was Eleazar Beall, too, who had foreseen Milbridge's emergence into a thriving and busy industrial city and had gone out into what was then the country, two miles from the tiny village of Milrock, and built —solidly, of brick and teakwood and cypress which would last forever—the Beall house. He had lived a long and busy life, keeping the reins of the Company in his own hands until the end.

Kirk's father's tenure had been brief and all but disastrous. It was during his lifetime, toward the end of it, that in the hope of restoring finances, Beall stock had gone for the first time outside the family. The resultant increase in capital had kept the works going but Kirk's father had by no means been the gifted and hard-hitting businessman that his grandfather had been; the business had not flourished. Indeed, during the years of Kirk's boyhood it had barely survived and there had been scarcely enough income to support Emily Beall, Clare and Kirk. But then Kirk, driving hard through school, spending every moment possible at the plant, had taken over the management and from that moment on things had been different. Kirk had been, as naturally he would be, Maggy thought with pride, spectacularly successful. There were new methods, new products, a reorganized and enlarged sales force, advertising, new business. Money rolled in, as Emily said, "hand over fist."

Maggy knew all that but there was much she didn't know. She said rather timidly, "I don't understand about the stock, Kirk."

He didn't smile indulgently and he didn't put her off. "It's simple. Up to now the Beall stock has been owned, and still is, largely by Cousin Emily, Clare and me, and some stockholders who bought blocks of stock during my father's lifetime. Well, the business is growing. So we want to get the stock on the open market, as a public issue. Then anyone can buy it. First we must get some reliable brokerage house or investment banker to act as the under-writer. Of course they will require a complete examination of the business. If they are satisfied, the next step is the submission of our report to the Securities and Exchange Commission. If all is approved then the stock will be eligible for sale to the public."

"The big board?" She knew, at least, what that meant.

"We're not up to that yet. We may be sometime. It's like this. There are various exchanges, as well as the over-the-counter market. Their requirements differ, but in order to get your stock accepted by any one of them you have to have so much specified capital—assets, buildings, cash, inventory, accounts receivable—all that. You have to be able to show a certain net income for the year. Family stock holdings are limited to certain percentages of the whole. There's no need to bother your head with all these technicalities. Anyhow, once the underwriter is satisfied of a sound and promising financial situation, the SEC must, after examination, give its approval. After that, the stock can be traded through any broker. We hope this year to be able to get under the wire. At first the stock will be sold over the counter; later, we hope, on an exchange. We are confident that once the stock is on the open market it will sell, increase in value and drive up the price. I am putting this in its simplest way. The point is money comes in. We use it for expansion. Expansion brings more money, pays the stockholders, and we keep on expanding. And that means for you, darling, anything you want. Furs, jewels, trips abroad . . ."

The fairy princess, she thought. "Heavens, Kirk, I don't need all those things!"

Kirk did not hear her. He was looking across the lawn, his face very still and intent, looking at nothing, yet she

22

knew that he was in fact looking into a glittering future. He was ambitious. Perhaps Cousin Emily had been right when she said he was touched with financial genius.

A light breeze touched her face and suddenly and disconcertingly seemed to bring with it the touch of Josh's mouth upon her own. For a second she really felt as if Kirk might sense something.

And that wouldn't do, she thought unexpectedly. A deep instinct told her that Kirk wouldn't recognize that absurd and surprised kiss for the slight and unimportant little spark of—well, affection, whatever anybody called it, that it was.

But Josh himself, and the preposterous things he had said, stubbornly came into her mind, too. He couldn't have meant what he said; he couldn't have been serious, even though for a moment he had sounded as if he meant it.

Even supposing, just for supposing, he did mean it, there was no possible reason for opposing her marriage. Certainly he had no quarrel with Kirk; probably they had seen each other rarely and then only in a casual and friendly way for years—since Josh himself had gone away to school. As certainly there was no ugly little incident in Kirk's life which might give Josh a reason for taking a stand against her marriage. If there had been she'd have known it. There were no secrets in Milrock. And besides, everyone knew and liked and, more important, respected Kirk Beall.

The only alternative reason she could then think of was that Josh fancied himself in love with her and he wasn't, really. He'd have laughed in her face at the idea. Yet he had said—as if he meant it—you can't marry Kirk. He's not the man for you. But Kirk was the man for her.

23

Kirk said, "What are you thinking about?"

It was as if he had read her mind. She said, startled, "I don't know! Nothing, really. You can hear the river from here but you can barely see it. Just the flashes of light through the trees."

"The shrubbery has grown too heavy. I haven't paid much attention to the old place. I'll have it all fixed up now. Any way you like it. The house, the grounds, everything. We'll do it all over. It's really an ugly house, you know. Built at the wrong period and built to last. But we'll do the best we can with it. What did Josh have to say?"

It was never any use trying to change the subject, not with Kirk. He never missed anything; he could pick things out of the air. She wished furiously that the Army had kept Josh just for another week; even for three more days. She said, "He's just out of the Army."

"So I gathered." Kirk leaned his black head back against the chair so his fine face was tilted toward the sky. He lazily watched a cloud which was touched to pink by the setting sun. A few shafts of golden light sifted through the trees and across the lawn, yet there was a hushed kind of stillness in the air as if a summer shower was hovering around somewhere. She glanced toward the south, and soft gray clouds were coming up above the rose-festooned tennis court. Through the trees the flashes of the river were still touched with gold and rose. Kirk said, "What's Josh going to do? Go back to his old job?"

"So he said."

"Baller and Yule, wasn't it?"

"I don't remember. Yes, I think so. It's a brokerage firm."

Kirk laughed shortly. "It's *the* brokerage firm. Investment house. Put it in a class with—oh, Morgan's. They must think pretty well of Josh to keep his job open for him. I don't remember just what he did."

"Neither do I."

Kirk didn't say anything for a moment. Music came from the library windows open on the north end of the terrace, piano music played by strong hands with rippling cascades. It was Clare, of course.

A very slight shadow crossed Kirk's face. It was not disapproval exactly, merely a kind of stillness. Then he returned to Josh. "How long has it been since you've seen Josh? Before this evening, I mean."

Oh, damn Josh! Maggy thought. But she had to reply; if she didn't Kirk would ask her in another way, in another way and another way, until she did reply. "It was just before my mother left for Paris. We had sold the house and were packing. I had come down from Boston to help. He came in and helped, too. He was home for the week end."

"Didn't he write to you while he was in the service?"

It was a light and casual question but she knew that she must reply to that, too. A telephone rang inside the house; the music broke off with a clatter, and something that wasn't a frown, that wasn't even a wrinkle between Kirk's black eyebrows, smoothed itself away. Maggy said, "No, he didn't write. . . . Kirk, it was wonderful to talk to my mother last night."

"We'll phone to her again if you like right after the wedding. . . . She sounded fine."

"She said you were keeping her room full of flowers."

"It's the least I could do. It seems too bad it happened like that. Not that Cousin Emily isn't enjoying taking over for your mother." He laughed softly.

Probably it was true. There had been a perfect flood of letters, cables and telephone calls flying back and forth between Emily in Milrock, and Cornelia Warren in Paris, mutual and delighted congratulations at first and then getting down to practical wedding arrangements. There had been, even, a little friendly bickering for Emily felt (spurred on secretly by Kirk, Maggy knew) that since most of the wedding guests were business friends of Kirk's, Emily (which meant Kirk) wished to pay for the wedding reception. Maggy had wondered just how Emily had worded her suggestion for she certainly hadn't said it baldly like that. Cornelia had put a stop to that with a decisive cable: "Darling can see straight through you believe me exchequer plentiful for my only childs wedding have cabled Jensens Catering let them know how many arrive New York two weeks before wedding I love you Warren."

And then, ironically, as she was pulling a suitcase down from a shelf, Cornelia had slipped. She telephoned from the American Hospital in Neuilly. It was so slight a fracture in one small vertebra that she could scarcely see it on the x-ray but she had to stay in the hospital and they were not to postpone the wedding, they were not to change anything. Kirk and Maggy were coming to Paris anyway, it was the first stop in that magnificent honeymoon—Paris, Rome, Madrid. Cornelia would see them the day after the wedding and she wouldn't hear of anything else.

Cornelia could be firm. Maggy, understanding her mother, had at last yielded. But perhaps, as Kirk said, Emily yielded the more readily because she really liked taking over for Maggy's mother. She was in her element; the smallest detail was important to her.

Kirk said now, quietly, "Maggy, you do understand

that any time you want money for your mother—any time now or in the future—you have only to tell me."

She was infinitely touched by it. She put out her hand toward Kirk but he was watching the cloud as it moved slowly toward the treetops, thrust along by the increasing mass of pearly gray pushing up from the south. She said, "She's independent; you know that. We made out for years on the government insurance and allowance and it was plenty—you know, my father was a captain when his ship was sunk. We had enough for our needs. And now that she's got a job she is putting away everything she can for a little nest egg. She used to send me money, too, while I was in training and she kept it up while I was working. I couldn't stop her. I put that away for her, too. But if she ever should need anything—you know what that means to me, Kirk. It's like you."

"She needn't keep on working at all if she doesn't want to."

"Oh, but she wants to."

"Yes. Yes, I understand. . . . Why didn't you say good-bye to Josh?

"*What?*"

"You didn't say a word. I invited him to our wedding. I invited him to come here tomorrow. You didn't say anything."

"But—but I . . ."

"I expected you to say something. The fact is—well, it's absurd of course—but it actually occurred to me that perhaps you and Josh had quarreled about something."

We *had* quarreled, Maggy thought, with a little flair of anger, which almost irresistibly impelled her to say it aloud—we had quarreled because he said I couldn't marry

27

you and he was only trying to tease me but he said it as if he meant it.

She wouldn't say it, of course. Kirk had a temper; she didn't know how she knew that but she knew it. Kirk wouldn't take it lightly and dismiss it as she had. She said, "I'm sorry. I just didn't think."

Kirk swung his legs around, sat up to face her and smiled so his whole face lit up. "We'll forget Josh. He's not important. You are. Three more days . . ."

He rose, came to her, took her hands and she lifted her face to him. But the door behind them clattered and Clare came out.

"Whoops—sorry. I didn't mean to disturb you two lovebirds. But guess what! We've got another wedding guest. Lydia Clowe is home."

THREE

Clare came around the chairs and perched herself in a flurry of wide, orange-colored skirts on the stone balustrade.

The sun had gone now and the clouds were welding themselves into a gray mass which was barely touched on the westward rim by a rosy glow left from the sunset. Somewhere near them a bird made a peculiarly busy and alert kind of chirp which as a child Maggy had called the robin's rain song. Kirk released her hand and strolled to the balustrade where he stood looking out again toward the river. "Really?" he said.

Clare nodded with a nervously energetic jerk of her head. She was framed as in a portrait by the greens of the foliage behind her; her angular face, her black hair, her thin bare arms and shoulders and orange-colored dress were all vividly outlined. There was a strong family resemblance between Clare and Kirk, brother and sister; they had the same black hair and startling light gray eyes between black eyelashes, the same strongly aquiline and decisive features. But the transmission of the same physical traits had undergone change between them; Kirk was almost spectacularly handsome in a masculine way. In Clare the decisive chin was a trifle too long and narrow; the high forehead a fraction too high and strained over the temples; her fine nose and high cheekbones were a little too fine and sharp; her red lipsticked mouth just a fraction too narrow and pinched. Her smallest motion was swift and tense. She saw the package of cigarettes which Kirk had left on the table, slid off the balustrade and jerked out a cigarette quickly, as if somebody might take it away from her.

She returned to perch on the balustrade. "She got home last night. She phoned just now."

Kirk said, "Oh. Josh Mason is at home, too."

Clare flicked ashes which had not had time to collect on her cigarette. "Have you seen Josh? Did you invite him to the wedding? Dr. Mason had a card but I didn't think of Josh. He was in Germany, wasn't he? He must be out of the Army."

Kirk nodded. "Just now. How is Lydia?"

"We didn't talk long. She's opened her house. Didn't George tell you she was coming home?"

"No, I don't think he did."

Maggy said idly, "Who is Lydia?"

Kirk turned. "Oh, my dear, I forgot you didn't know her. She's lived here only since her marriage. She is George Clowe's wife."

George Clowe was by profession a lawyer but he worked for Kirk. He was a round, bouncing, nearly bald, highly colored man in his thirties who obviously respected Kirk and Kirk obviously respected him. What exactly he did for the Company, Maggy didn't know; he seemed to be a kind of all-around adviser, a first mate to Kirk's captaincy. Clare said to Maggy, "They closed their house here in Milrock—it's on the other side of town—when Lydia went abroad. George took a room over in Milbridge to be near the works. She's been away—how long, Kirk?"

"I don't remember. Three months—four."

"Three months at least. She's been all over everywhere. She had a long stay in Puerto Rico. . . . She'd already heard about the wedding."

"I expect George told her," Kirk said and looked at his watch.

"No, the express man told her the minute she got to town. She asked me about it and about Maggy, of course." Clare gave Maggy a sudden, flashing smile which had some of Kirk's charm. "I told her you were a beauty, Maggy. . . . I thought it would do her good. She's been the beauty of the place ever since she married George. Then I told her that George had already done his full duty with a wedding present. More than his full duty," Clare said with an edge in her voice. "Another enormous silver pitcher! Just like George. Perfectly conventional and no imagination. He's been in this house hundreds of times and still didn't see that the house is bulging with silver. I am glad you'll have to see to it all, Maggy. I've had enough of it."

"You can take anything you want to your own house, you know, Clare," said Kirk turning away from the terrace.

Clare seemed to think for a moment.

"All right. Maggy and I will go over things. I would like the piano, if you don't mind, Maggy."

"Why, of course," Maggy said. "Anything you want. There must be some other things you have some special— oh, sentimental attachment for—anything you want."

Kirk laughed. "Clare is not very sentimental." He looked at his watch again. "It's after six."

"Oh!" Maggy got quickly to her feet, guiltily aware of her wrinkled shorts and limp white shirt. "I must go and change."

31

Kirk held the door open for her and leaned over to kiss her lightly as she went into the big living room where, now, tables were stretched all along one wall and laden with wedding presents. The room was in shadow. The crystal and china and silver caught what light there was and winked through the dusk.

Emily had given Maggy the big guest room directly above the terrace and overlooking the lawn, the thick line of trees and shrubbery and, at that height, a long stretch of the Matoax. Maggy went to the bay window. Beyond the trees the river had already turned a still gray which masked its deep current. The rather eerie light of the coming storm seemed to make everything more vivid so the old landing, the silvery-looking canoe, and the tennis court with its high fence heavy with roses seemed very clear and vivid. The lawn was bright green. The roses looked even redder. She turned away from the window.

Her wedding dress hung over a closet door on a padded hanger and in the soft light was misty and ethereal as a cloud. Her mother had sent it to her. She had already tried it on with Clare and Emily watching; together they had taken it from the two enormous packages which had arrived from Paris. Maggy had scarcely believed her own image in the mirror with the soft folds of white silk fitting closely at throat and waist and then billowing out in wide swirls. The veil was gathered into a close little cap of lace. "That's real lace," Emily had said, adjusted her spectacles, peered more closely and added, "it's rose point! Cornelia must have paid a fortune for this."

She hadn't; she had made that clear. "They promised to get your wedding dress off today," she had written to Maggy. "It really is a dream. But don't worry. It didn't cost much. That's one of the perks of fashion scouting. My feet may ache but I can dress for next to nothing. Everything else for your trousseau will be waiting for you here. Darling, I wish I had not been so stupid as to twist my aging back. I can't wait to see you. What fun we'll have."

Maggy turned on the shower, dressed hurriedly and went downstairs where Emily stood in the middle of the living room, a worried look in her vague blue eyes and a list in her hand.

"Dear," she said, "we'd better give all these another check. Everybody Kirk knows seems to have sent a wedding present, and it would be dreadful if we missed one." Her eyes focused on Maggy. "What a charming outfit! Did your mother send you that from Paris, too?"

Maggy laughed. "New York. Fourteen ninety-five plus tax."

Emily eyed the thin, full-skirted cotton dress, black but frosted with blue and white so it looked cool, and the high-heeled piqué slippers which Maggy had had dyed black. Everything pleased Emily. She smiled. "Kirk is getting a thrifty wife. He's at the phone. We'll have dinner a little early so Mrs. Elwell can get away. Clare and Alroy won't be home for dinner. She went to Milbridge to meet Alroy and they are going to look at a house which has just come on the market. I did have a pencil somewhere here. . . ."

She began to search the table in a worried way.

Emily Beall was really a large woman, big-boned and well fleshed; she always seemed small and very feminine with her gray curls, her anxious blue eyes and an air of worried uncertainty. She found a pencil and went to one of the long tables. "So many things!" she sighed. Her

33

plump figure in its white linen dress moved tentatively along the table. She paused to thump a huge glass punch bowl with an experimental forefinger. It gave forth a clear ring and Emily nodded. "Lovely. But really, when will you use it?"

"When the Hally Brass Company comes to dinner."

Emily was extremely literal; she gave Maggy a startled glance. "Dear, they employ twelve thousand . . ." She caught the laugh in Maggy's eyes, stopped, and smiled uncertainly.

"We'll check every fork," Maggy said with compunction. "You've got the list. Ready? A dozen goblets from Mr. and Mrs. Albert Willard . . ."

"Willard Chemical Company." Emily made a check.

Kirk came from the telephone in the library. He gave Emily sherry and Maggy a long, cool drink, smoked and watched them. Dinner was served actually a little before seven to accommodate Mrs. Elwell who lived in the village and whose husband picked her up at the gate promptly at eight. He also picked up Mildred, a girl who had been employed as extra help during the hurried and busy days before the wedding.

After dinner Emily, Maggy and Kirk sat over coffee for a long time on the terrace; when the rain clouds grew so low that they could almost be felt like a tangible presence overhead, and at last the rain began in a soft, light sprinkle, they went inside. "Darling," Emily said to Maggy, "I *would* feel better if we got entirely through the list. There will be more presents tomorrow, you know. How are you getting along with your notes?"

There had been discussion about that, too. Clare was all for printed cards of acknowledgment stating merely that a gift had arrived and a letter would be written later. Emily held out for handwritten letters of thanks but they must be written promptly. Therefore, she urged, if Maggy wrote as many letters as she could now it would save time later. "You can sign your married name, you know, after the wedding," she argued.

She had supplied Maggy with stacks of writing paper. But after several attempts to project herself into the future and write "Kirk and I thank you so much for the beautiful silver compote . . ." Maggy gave up and hid the note paper.

She said now, "Slowly . . ."

Kirk laughed, kissed the top of Emily's shining gray curls and took the tray of coffee cups into the house. "I've got work to do, too," he said. As Maggy and Emily went slowly along the table checking addresses, finding one or two errors, Maggy heard him in the library dictating into a machine—notes and letters, probably, designed to cover every possible contingency which could arise during his absence. Four weeks, Maggy thought with utter incredulity, four weeks of travel, new sights, new worlds—as Mrs. Kirk Beall. "Oh, dear," Emily said, "Clare put down that cocktail shaker from the Evanses in Milbridge and I do believe—yes, I'm sure it came from somebody in Detroit—I saw the card—now let me see . . ."

The sprinkle turned into a quiet rain, pattering on the terrace. They hadn't finished by eleven, but Emily was tired and sent Maggy to bed. Kirk heard them in the hall and came out. When Emily's back was turned as she fussed with the night lock on the front door, he took Maggy in his arms and kissed her hard.

She tingled as she went up the stairs. It was odd, she thought as she closed the door of the guest room, that she knew Kirk so well, yet when he took her like that in his arms, she was half afraid and a little shy as if he were a stranger.

She lay awake for a long time, in the enormous bed, listening to the sound of the rain on the terrace. It must have been very late when she awakened with a kind of start and a moment of bewilderment, finding herself in a strange bed, a strange room, and dreaming of roses.

It had been a frightening dream in which the roses seemed to become enormous and threatening creatures, big and red and growling like animals in a jungle, shooting out strangling holds everywhere, encroaching steadily upon her as if they had some secret purpose. She sat up, her heart racing. Somebody, sometime had said, ". . . scream . . . and nothing but the roses would hear you."

Then she heard the rain like soft footsteps on the terrace. She saw the dim outlines of her wedding dress. She lay back. An absurd dream!

It was due to Josh, of course. Josh had said something —what was it? Yes—"You could scream here until you were blue in the face and nothing but the roses would hear you."

Josh, she thought, with a little stab of irritation. It wasn't like Josh to say things like that! As if he could stop the wedding! Events were rolling on, all their wheels meshing and gathering momentum. Nothing in the world could stop them. Certainly not Josh.

But the uneasy dream still held her. She got out of bed and without turning on the light crossed to the big bay windows which she had half lowered on account of the rain. She pulled one of them up as far as it would go, and the fresh moist air touched her face. As she stood there she heard, distantly, a car spattering gravel; the sound came

36

from the south end of the house where the driveway curved in from the road, turned past the house and went on to the garage. The sound diminished and stopped. It was probably Alroy and Clare returning so it wasn't as late as it had seemed. She didn't hear the front door open or close; she heard no footsteps on the stairs but they would know that the house was asleep; they would be very quiet.

The rain drummed softly on the terrace below, and on the whole house, the river, the trees—and the roses. When she slept again she didn't dream anything; indeed, she slept so late that by the time she got downstairs Kirk and Alroy had already gone to Milbridge and the works. The rain had stopped and the whole world glittered. A caterer's truck stood at the open front door, cases of champagne blocked the door to the dining room, and the hall was stacked with tables and chairs. Clare sat on the bottom steps of the stairs, holding a cup of coffee, and Emily was all but wringing her hands. "Good morning, dear," she said to Maggy. "Kirk has gone to the office. He said not to wake you. Clare, *what* shall we do with all these tables?"

"Put them in the library. The ice-cream chairs, too. Maggy, let's have our breakfast on the terrace. The dining-room table is stacked with china."

The day was a stepped-up version of the previous day. It was hot, clear and still, with the wheels of the wedding preparations going faster and faster—almost, Maggy thought once, as if the whole intricate machine were going down a long slope with no brakes, accelerating with every inexorable second. There were last-minute acceptances; there were prolonged telephone calls to the caterers in New York; there was a frenzy of house cleaning.

There were errands to Milrock—Clare's dress, which she had insisted was too long and over Emily's protests had taken to the village dressmaker to be shortened, was still not ready. The Milrock Inn, which perched on the very edge of the river a few miles northward, did not have enough rooms for the guests who, now, were to stay all night; rooms had to be found for the overflow and complex plans made to turn Maggy's room and Kirk's room into guest rooms the instant they had taken their departure after the reception, to go to the airport. A hitch developed about the time for the rehearsal in the church and it had to be postponed to the late afternoon before the wedding, which upset Emily. There were more wedding presents to be unpacked, set up suitably and listed. Store cupboards were rummaged; great stacks of china and glasses and silver had to be washed till they glittered.

Maggy didn't go to the lookout point that day. There wasn't time but she wouldn't have gone anyway. It was after four when Emily said exhaustedly that they couldn't do any more that day. "You girls go straight and clean up. You look like chimney sweeps."

"Excelsior sweeps," Maggy said and plucked a shred of excelsior from Clare's tousled mass of black hair.

"Next time," Clare said, "you'd better elope. I did."

Emily's pale blue eyes instantly were troubled. Maggy said, "There won't be a next time."

Kirk and Alroy came home while Maggy was getting into a fresh dress, a thin white cotton with a scarlet belt and scarlet sandals. They brought George Clowe home with them. Maggy heard Kirk call him from the hall. "Get out some cold drinks, George. Make yourself at home. I'll be down as soon as I've had a shower."

But when Maggy went downstairs, through the living

room and out to the terrace, Josh was sitting like a rock in one of the green-canvased chairs.

"Oh!" Maggy said.

The barest flicker of amusement touched Josh's face. Then he rose. "I want to talk to you."

And all at once again he looked different; he looked as he had looked when he greeted Kirk the day before—older somehow, more matured, a little remote and yet curiously alert and watchful. Maggy put her hands on the back of the nearest chair. "No!"

"But Maggy . . ." The door opened and George came out, carrying a tray that tinkled with glasses.

"Hello, Maggy," he said. "How's our bride? I'll just put this on the table. . . ."

Josh turned to the table and swept off newspapers. George put down the tray. "What will you have, Maggy?"

George, his face red with heat, his bald head shining below wisps of light hair, began to sort out tall glasses and fill them with ice. He had removed his coat and loosened his collar and tie. "Hot today," he said. "Tom Collins all right for you, Maggy? How about you, Josh?"

Josh brought her the tall glass. One reason why he looked so different, she thought, was the way he was dressed. His faded khakis had seemed natural and like Josh. He now wore gray slacks and a navy blue linen coat and looked rather elegant and muscularly hard and trim in contrast to George's plump and perspiring figure.

"Let's go up to the lookout point," Josh said, his hazel eyes intent. "The others aren't down yet. George can do with a rest. . . ."

"No." Maggy took the glass gingerly so her fingers wouldn't touch Josh's brown hand, and placed it beside her.

George was clattering ice at the table. Josh said in a low voice, "Oh Maggy, you *are* a baby! I am going to talk to you whether you want to or not. Come on . . ."

He was quite capable of taking her by the arm and dragging her off the terrace. She took a firm, defensive hold on the arms of her chair and Josh saw it. He laughed softly but there was a determined light in his hazel eyes. He took a quick step toward her and Emily came out of the house, fresh in one of her embroidered linen dresses, and said, "Josh, my dear! How nice!"

Josh's face cleared. He went to kiss Emily's faintly powdered cheek. She held him away from her and looked him over deliberately.

Josh's eyes twinkled. "Everything all right, ma'am?"

"I think so. I really think so," Emily said approvingly and put one hand on his shoulder.

It seemed to touch a depth in Josh. He loved Emily and he loved Maggy's mother, who had in their different ways looked after a motherless boy. He said soberly, "Thank you, Miss Emily."

The door banged again and Clare came out in a flurry of green skirts, kissed Josh and cried, "You look marvelous! I'll have—oh, a long drink, George, with lots of lemon. Josh, you got home just in time for the wedding."

Alroy Fisher came from the house, too, so quietly that Maggy was not aware of it until he loomed up beside her, enormous and very much the gentleman of leisure in white slacks and a pale blue, meticulously tailored linen coat. He shook hands with Josh in the rather overdone manner with which Alroy invested his slightest courtesy, but briefly and absently, too, for his slate-colored eyes were fixed on the cocktail table. He scarcely listened to Josh's reply but dropped his hand at once and made for the table where he mixed a pitcher of martinis and gulped one down thirstily, without waiting for it to chill. He then sat down, holding the pitcher and stirring its contents.

Maggy eyed her prospective brother-in-law with a little flicker of uncertainty. She knew him actually very slightly but she was not attracted by what she knew. He was a handsome (and, Maggy suspected, lazy) Carolinian, transplanted to New York; if he had had a profession or any kind of job when Clare married him, Maggy did not know what it was. There was a hovering impression that Alroy had been born with, at least, a silver spoon in his handsome mouth but if so the spoon had not been very durable, for after only a year or so of marriage, Clare and Alroy had returned to live in the Beall house, with Cousin Emily and Kirk, and Alroy was working, or presumed to be working, in the Beall Company—something in the financial end, she thought. He was undoubtedly handsome, with classical features and a big fair head which seemed somehow just a little larger than life; he was a big man, too; tall, a little too fleshy and slack, yet imposing. Maggy could not account for her faint dislike in any specific way; perhaps it was due as much as anything to the curiously boding and sullen look his handsome, fair face could take on—and the way his slate-colored eyes seemed to watch everything and everybody. He sat now, looking down into the pitcher of martinis and, Maggy was perfectly sure, not missing a word that anybody said.

Not that anybody was saying anything in particular even though everybody except Alroy seemed to be talking. Maggy did not know that Kirk had come from the house until she felt his hand on her chin, turning her face upward to him.

He kissed her slowly, prolonging it a little, which as a

41

rule Kirk did not do when others were present. She knew that Josh was watching and felt her face grow pink. But when Kirk released her she glanced quickly at Josh and he was replying to something Alroy had said about the works. "I haven't visited there for years," Josh said. "I hear you've been going great guns."

Kirk was in an unusually exuberant mood. "Come and see," he said. "Come over—well, you'll have to make it tomorrow. I'd like to show you around myself. . . . What have you got there, George?"

George, though, had sunk down into a long chair and was mopping his red face. Kirk mixed his own drink deftly as he did everything. Clare settled on the balustrade again, her bare tanned legs dangling. Alroy filled another glass, put back his fair head, and downed the martini. "Ah—I've been looking forward to this all day. Come on, Josh, and take a look at the works. Kirk wants to show you around himself because you may be getting a chunk of our stock to sell one of these days. You're with Baller and Yule, aren't you?"

Josh nodded. "Does that mean you are getting out a new stock issue?"

For no reason Maggy looked at him sharply but there was nothing to see—only Josh sitting with one long leg crossed over the other, holding a glass in his hand and looking at Alroy with a kind of impersonal politeness. She couldn't imagine why she felt that he was as alert as a hunter listening for some rustle in the undergrowth.

Kirk gave Alroy one clear, cool look, then laughed lightly and sat down. "Nothing to set the world on fire, Josh. We're a small concern, you know."

Alroy's big, regular features were suddenly a little sullen as if Kirk's look had been a repressive one. Josh said, turning his glass in his hands, that he'd like very much to see the works. "Everybody says you are really doing wonders, Kirk."

"We've been lucky," Kirk said. "It's a prosperous period. Alroy's getting a little ahead of himself—or us, rather. But expansion does seem to be indicated. Right, George?"

George had put away his handkerchief, picked up a newspaper and was fanning himself. He gave a little start. "Oh, yes. Yes, certainly." His eyes went beyond Kirk, fixed and widened. He gave a kind of gulp and clumsily started to get out of his chair as Clare, looking down toward the end of the terrace, cried, "Lydia!"

Everybody turned to look. A woman and a man were coming up the steps at the south end of the terrace. "Hello, everybody," the woman said gaily. "We left Ralph's car in the driveway and came around the end of the house. We knew you'd be here on the terrace."

"Lydia!" Emily cried and rose to meet her.

There was a little hubbub of greeting. Somewhere behind Maggy a door closed softly.

Clare introduced her. "Maggy, this is Lydia. Kirk's bride, Lydia."

"How do you do?" Lydia said.

She gave Maggy one swift bright look from eyes that were brilliantly, almost stonily blue and turned instantly to Emily. She was a beauty as Clare had said, with flawlessly regular features, a round firm chin and a rose-petal complexion. Her golden hair was cut thickly, parted on one side and waved back in an oddly old-fashioned way, but not a hair was out of place. Her pale pink lipstick matched her pale pink dress, which stretched only a little too tightly over opulent but decorously restrained curves.

Her teeth were so white and even that her smile looked oddly cold. Kirk said, "And here is Ralph, Maggy. But of course you know Ralph Hewitt."

"Why, yes. How do you do, Ralph?" Maggy put out her hand and Ralph Hewitt took it briefly and as always with Ralph, rather awkwardly. He seemed a kind of dim and shriveled train to Lydia's dazzling, blonde comet; he wore a wrinkled brown seersucker suit and dabbed at his bony, freckled forehead nervously as he spoke to Emily and told George with what seemed a burst of daring that he'd take bourbon and branch water. Ralph, too, was a lawyer; he had set up his office on Milrock's main street, in the front room of a white clapboard house; he lived a bachelor existence in the back of the house and, Maggy suspected, spent most of his time watching people come and go along Main Street, waiting for somebody to stop to see him with a will to be drawn up or a real estate transfer to be made.

Emily looked around vaguely and said, "Where's George? Why he was here just a moment ago. . . ."

Lydia sat down; she drew her pink skirt modestly around her legs and looked at Emily. "I'd better get it over with, Miss Emily," she said clearly but with the utmost composure. "George and I were divorced last month."

It was so still for a moment that Maggy could hear the soft murmur of the river.

Then Clare said, shrilly, "Why, what a surprise!"

She couldn't be laughing, Maggy thought quickly. Yet there was something very bright in her gray eyes.

Emily sat down with the effect of a collapse. "Oh dear! Oh, dear me—but you both *must* come to the wedding!"

FOUR

Clare, then, did laugh, a short little gasp which she didn't try to conceal. Lydia gave her a cold, bright glance. Kirk came forward easily and poured a drink for Ralph, who was fidgeting with his collar. "Bourbon you said, didn't you, Ralph?"

Clare said, "But nobody knew it! Kirk, why didn't you tell us?"

Kirk shrugged. "What will you have to drink, Lydia?"

Clare persisted. "But Kirk, didn't George tell you?"

"No," Kirk said briefly.

Emily eyed Lydia worriedly. "My dear, why didn't you tell us? We didn't know . . ."

"Nobody knew," Lydia said coolly. "There was no reason to make a fuss about it. I'll have iced tea, Kirk, if there is any."

It diverted Emily. "Oh dear—I'm afraid—I didn't think about iced tea. I knew the men would want . . ."

"It doesn't matter," Lydia said. "Give me what everybody else is having, Kirk. Except . . ." Her brilliant eyes took in Alroy, still standing with the martini in his hand, watching her. A look of distaste came into Lydia's lovely face. "Except a martini. How you can drink those things in weather like this, Alroy!"

"Nothing like it," Alroy said defiantly and downed another.

45

Emily said vaguely, "I'd better go—I've got to see about . . ." and went into the house.

Clare's thin mouth was really smiling now. "She's going to talk to George. You upset her, Lydia. She's thinking about the wedding. Afraid you and George will hurl punch bowls at each other."

Josh was standing beside Maggy, his hazel eyes taking in everything. There was again something rather watchful, yet unnaturally polite about him.

Lydia said to Clare, "Don't be absurd!"

And Josh said, "Didn't you say something about tennis, Kirk?"

"Tennis!" Alroy groaned. "On a day like this!"

Kirk laughed. "A good idea. Come on, Alroy. Work off some of that extra poundage. How about it, everybody? The court's not in very good shape. Walt was edging the driveway today and didn't have time to roll it. But we might have some doubles. The net's up . . ."

"Sagged all to hell," Alroy said.

"Walt spent most of the day polishing Maggy's new car," Clare said. "Come on everybody—bring your glasses. Ralph, yours needs sweetening."

"Oh, no, no," Ralph protested but lingered with Clare at the table for a moment, talking, while the others strolled down the steps to the flagstone path. At the tennis court Clare and Ralph caught up with them and sent Alroy to the garage for rackets and balls and extra tennis shoes for Josh and Ralph.

But once arrived at the long, weather-beaten benches and table which stood beside the tennis court, Ralph demurred. "Too hot," he said and eyed the river, which close at hand now looked cool and sparkling. He strolled down toward the landing.

What happened then was not very clear, ever. Clare drew Maggy to a seat on the bench. Kirk and Lydia wandered on with Ralph. Alroy presently came along the path from the garage with tennis rackets under his arm and Josh began to tighten the net. Alroy dropped the rackets on the bench and went to help him. It was Alroy who paused to mop his forehead, glanced at the river and said, "For God's sake, they're taking out the canoe."

Maggy turned to look. Lydia was already seated in the canoe as decorously as if she were at a ball, with the sun making a nimbus of light around her blonde hair and her skirt tucked in around her legs. Ralph crawled rather gingerly into the stern seat and took a paddle. Kirk untied the canoe, glanced up at Maggy with a kind of a smiling shrug as if hospitality required too much of him, and took the middle seat and the other paddle. Alroy said, "If I were Kirk, nobody would get me out in that canoe! Not with the river as high as it is this year."

Maggy glanced at him, surprised, and he gave the net another tug, lounged over to the bench, mopped his forehead and said, "Kirk can't swim. Didn't you know that?"

"Oh . . ." Maggy did remember then; when she was a child and her mother brought her to visit Emily, they would often swim—her mother and Emily, Josh if he happened to be there and sometimes Clare—but Kirk would watch them or bat tennis balls against the high backstop. There was a big rock perhaps twenty feet out from the landing and it had marked the limits for Maggy. She could paddle or, as she grew taller, wade out to the rock; after that, somebody—her mother or Emily or Josh —had to be with her. It was a rule for beyond the smooth big rock the water was deep and cold. She looked down at the river again, searching for the rock but the water was too high; it had completely covered the big rock. The canoe glided gently away from the landing and the willows around it and into the sun.

Josh came from the other end of the net and paused to watch the canoe.

Alroy sighed. "Are you sure you want a game, Josh? I'm about beat with this heat."

Josh laughed a little but a gleam of purpose came into his eyes again. He picked up the glass he had set on the table near the bench. "As a matter of fact, I'd like to take a look at the Matoax from the old arbor and the lookout point. How about it, Maggy?"

Maggy was on her feet before she realized that she had moved. "I've got to pack . . ." she said and walked quickly away and up the flagstone path toward the house.

It was abrupt. She could feel Clare's surprised and questioning glance follow her. But then she heard Alroy say lazily, "Hot up there at the lookout point, too. Right in the sun. Josh, have you seen the new car that Kirk got for Maggy?"

That was all Maggy heard. But she wasn't going up to the old arbor with Josh.

She crossed the terrace, her heels making soft little thuds of sound. The chairs were gay with their green and white cushions. It was shady there with only the gleams of the river showing through the silvery green willows. She went into the house and through the long living room. Emily and George were in the library. She heard voices and a few clear words as she went up the stairs. "Well—of course there was nothing else to do. But I do think you might have told us, George," Emily said.

George said, "Lydia didn't want anybody to know until

it was over. You know how Lydia is—conventional—hates talk . . ."

Maggy went quickly on up the wide, dark stairway. It was dusky now all along the east side of the house with its windows heavily draped in vines but in her room on the west side there was a burst of sunlight. Whether or not Josh had been serious the day before there was something unmistakably purposeful and intent in his attitude now. She was sure that he had intended to get her away from the others and tell her all over again that she was not to marry Kirk. There was no possible reason for it; he had got some notion into his stubborn, sandy head but she wasn't going to listen to him.

She really ought to start to pack. Emily had been fidgeting a little about that, too; Maggy mustn't pack so soon that her clothes would be irretrievably wrinkled, yet she mustn't leave packing till the very last.

Not that there was much to pack. She had bought only a few things—a suit of travel silk, which looked like tweed, to wear on the plane; an enveloping dark blue silk coat and a hat which was a velvet bow and a piece of veiling and nothing else. She looked at the hat doubtfully, wondering if it were sufficiently bridal.

And suddenly she arrived at the reason for Josh's opposition to her marriage. It was perfectly clear and simple. The news of her marriage had really been news to Josh. It had come to him unexpectedly, out of the blue, without any preparation for it. He had known that her mother was away. So, without intending to, perhaps without knowing it, Josh had slid into the role of a relative whose plain duty it was to make certain that a projected marriage was likely to be a happy and successful one. He had taken the first, surprised line a brother or father might and often did take, and opposed it. It was perfectly clear and logical and that was all there was to it. So she needn't have run away from him.

A big leather handbag, which was large enough to hold essentials for a plane trip, stood on a chest of drawers. The nurses at the hospital had clubbed together to present it to her as a wedding present. It was a handsome bag; she opened it, thinking with gratitude and with a little pang of nostalgia of all the bus rides and movies the price of the handbag represented. It had a waterproof lining and spaces for plastic jars and bottles. She hadn't placed it on the tables with the other wedding presents; for one thing it would have been swamped by all that glittering show and for another thing she had wanted to keep it close to her, affectionately. She took up one of the bottles. Perfume? Hand lotion? What?

Now that she understood Josh's motive it might be better to go downstairs, find him and get everything clear between them.

She would like to feel, while she stood there in the little church being married to Kirk, that Josh was there, too, approving her marriage, backing her up, proud of her as the family she didn't have might have been.

She put down the bottle, went over to the bay window and looked down. The terrace directly below was bright and gay with color but no one was there. She could see the benches beside the tennis court and nobody was there either.

As she looked, the canoe, which had apparently been edging along the shore, came out from beyond the rim of willows and headed toward the middle of the river. Lydia was still sitting, facing the house, as the canoe moved over the sun-dappled water. Ralph's thin back swayed as he paddled. The sunlight was dazzling. Kirk seemed to turn as if to speak to Ralph. One of the paddles, Kirk's, was suspended in the air, drops from it making a tiny cascade which glittered in the bright light.

Maggy went back to the table, dropped the plastic bottle into the handbag, started for the door, and somebody screamed. It was a shrill, wild scream of terror. She ran back to the window.

Where there had been a canoe gliding quietly along, there was now a wild flurry of water. The canoe had overturned and was floating upside down in the river. Through the commotion around it she saw Lydia's head rising, dripping with water. Ralph and Kirk were thrashing about near the canoe. A bright orange spot bobbed between them. Lydia screamed again.

Maggy whirled and ran—down the stairs, through the shadowy living room out to the terrace. It seemed to take forever. She saw and heard no one. Lydia screamed again.

Maggy stumbled down the steps from the terrace and ran along the flagstone path to the landing. As she ran, she heard footsteps pounding along behind her. Josh passed her, tearing off his coat.

FIVE

By the time Maggy reached the little landing, Josh had jerked off his shoes and was wading out through the rocky shallows.

Alroy came puffing along, making the old planks shake. He paused to pull off his shoes and then swung himself down into the water.

Clare shrieked from behind her. "Turn on your back—Lydia—turn on your back and float . . ."

Josh had reached the deep water and plunged into it, swimming strongly. Alroy dipped down like a porpoise, his arms flailing. Maggy didn't know that she was snatching off her own sandals until Clare's strong hand came down hard on her shoulder. "You can't swim in that current. Besides, Ralph will get them out. He's an expert swimmer." She screamed, *"Float*—Lydia—turn on your back . . ."

Lydia had drifted away from the canoe—or the canoe, caught in the current, had drifted swiftly away from her. Ralph and Kirk still made a splashing, flailing commotion near the canoe. Lydia's arms were flailing the water helplessly, too. "She's panicked," Clare cried. "Damn fool. She's lost her head."

Alroy lifted his big face, seemed to take a line which would meet the canoe and swam toward it but a little down river, allowing for the current to bring the canoe across his course. The sun was glaring upon the water, dazzling their eyes. Lydia's head looked small and incredibly far away. But Josh was nearing her.

The canoe swirled farther out into the river. Someone, either Kirk or Ralph, had got hold of it—must have got hold of it for Maggy could see a head traveling along with the canoe. Clare said, "It's—yes, it's Kirk. He'll be all right if he hangs on. The current comes in toward the bank further down. . . . Alroy," she called out over the water. She waved her arms and pointed toward the splashing commotion around Lydia. "Lydia!" she screamed. "Lydia!"

Alroy didn't hear. He was still making slowly but steadily for the canoe. Apparently Kirk saw what was happening. One arm came up in an imperative wave back toward Lydia. He shouted something at Alroy and Alroy heard that for he took another survey of the river, shouted, "Okay," and headed up river for Lydia and Josh. It was all so slow—so slow, Maggy thought. Then Clare shaded her eyes with her hand and cried, "There—Josh has almost reached her. Oh Lord, she's fighting him."

Lydia *was* fighting. Josh seemed to try to argue with her. He had her by the arm. The two heads, wet and shiny in the sun, bobbed up and down. Lydia struggled wildly and all at once Josh's fist flashed.

Maggy couldn't see what happened but Clare said, "Good. He's knocked her out. Only thing to do."

We need a boat, Maggy thought. They'll never get her to shore. The current is too strong. She looked wildly about and the rowboat was still upside down a few feet away, beside the landing.

"Let's take the rowboat," she cried but again Clare stopped her.

"It's no use. Hasn't been in the water this year and it's full of leaks anyway. There. Josh is floating Lydia."

He was making slow progress, pulling Lydia along with him, fighting the current. Alroy was still some distance away but heading for Lydia and Josh. The sun on the water was so glaring and bright that everything seemed to dance around them.

The canoe though was now drifting closer toward the shore, south beyond the landing. Kirk's black head was beside it and Maggy could see it clearly now. He had one arm linked somehow over the canoe. A bright orange dot bobbed in the wake of the canoe. It was, she saw then, a cushion, probably a kapok-filled cushion from the canoe, intended as a life preserver.

The bank south of the landing was low and crowded with shrubbery. The canoe was heading directly for it so Kirk was safe, or would be in another moment or two. Alroy had reached Josh and Lydia. There was again a kind of commotion in the water; then Maggy could see that Alroy and Josh had got Lydia between them and were returning. Emily said behind her, panting as if she had been running, "It's such a long way. . . ."

Maggy had not been conscious of her approach. Clare said suddenly, "It's too much for them. Alroy is not a strong swimmer, no wind . . ." She swirled around, jerked off her slippers, sat down on the landing and swung her feet into the water. Maggy tugged the zipper on her dress, with its full and entangling white skirt, dropped the dress on the landing and pushed out of her own slippers. The water felt icy as it always had when she was a child. She groped for the slippery rocks. The thing to do was to wade out to the big rock and then plunge into the water. Clare was wading ahead of her, holding up her bright green dress, but Maggy reached the edge of the deep water first, took a long breath and launched herself into it. She wasn't a strong swimmer but she could keep herself afloat.

The current though, even there, was stronger than she had expected. She resorted instinctively to the safe, slow dog paddle she had first learned as a child. But she couldn't reach Josh and Lydia at that rate and the strength of the current was frightening. Clare came up beside her and lifted a wet face and streaming, flattened black hair. "They're all right," she gasped. "Come on back. The current's too strong. They're all right. . . ."

By that time Maggy had scarcely breath and strength enough to lift her own head and try to see across the dazzling path of the sun. But it *was* all right; Josh and Alroy, pulling Lydia between them, were nearing the bank rimmed with willows, north of the landing.

Clare's strong hand caught Maggy's bare shoulder. "Turn around! Kirk is all right, too. The canoe has drifted in close enough so he could get to shore."

They paddled back together slowly until they could feel rocks under their feet.

The canoe now was floating on down the river, swinging out away from the willows, but Kirk was on the bank scrambling through the undergrowth. He paused to shout at them. Maggy couldn't hear what he said.

Emily pulled her and Clare up to the landing. "I'll get the doctor," she said, and the planks thudded as she ran heavily toward the path.

Josh and Alroy had hauled Lydia up among the willows. Josh turned Lydia over on her face and stood astride her, pumping his hands up and down against her back.

Maggy scrambled her way toward them through willows that whipped her wet face. Alroy had crawled up a little from the bank and lay flat and sodden, gasping for breath. Maggy reached Josh and Lydia. "Here—I can do that, Josh. . . ."

Josh squatted down beside Lydia as Maggy took his place, her hands at Lydia's waist. Pump air in, pause a little, pump air out.

But Lydia was breathing steadily. Maggy felt the slow rise and fall and sought for Lydia's wrist. The pulse was strong and a little fast. Her eyelids fluttered and opened. Her eyes were blue and blank, staring at the sky and the trees above her. She gave a kind of shudder and said, clearly, "He tried to kill me."

Josh jerked forward. "Lydia! What did you say?"

Her blank, pale face didn't change. She stared at the sky for another second or two and then closed her eyes.

"Lydia!" Josh caught her shoulder and shook it. "Lydia —who tried to kill you?"

She didn't answer; she wouldn't answer. Her lips were as pale and set as stone.

Josh waited. Then slowly his hand left her shoulder, he lifted his head and gave Maggy a long, blazing look.

Kirk came plunging through the willows. "Is she all right?" he cried. Lydia still would not open her eyes. Maggy said, "Yes—yes—she's all right," but nobody heard it for Clare's high-pitched voice came from the landing. "Where's Ralph? Ralph . . ."

Josh pulled himself up and started, running, toward the landing. Kirk wheeled around, shouted to Maggy, "See to Lydia," and ran after him. Alroy had heard Clare, heaved himself up and plunged heavily toward the landing, too.

Lydia gave a shuddering sigh and retched. Maggy held her and watched the men through the long green and gold streamers of the willows.

They got out the rowboat. They lugged it to the water, dropped it down and apparently it began to fill at once. They seemed to debate, staring up and down the river, searching the glaring, moving currents, shading their eyes. There seemed to be some debate, too, about venturing into the river again, swimming. Alroy shrugged his big shoulders and seemed about to wade out through the shallows. Josh stopped him with an imperative gesture. Then Kirk started for the house, running wearily. Josh and Alroy disappeared into the undergrowth on the other side of the landing, thrashing through the heavy laurels. Clare's thin green figure was sharply defined as she stood still on the landing, her wet dress clinging to her, her hands shielding her eyes from the sun's glare.

Lydia mumbled something and got up on her hands and knees and then groggily, as Maggy helped her, to her feet. She swayed for a moment; then she turned without a word and started walking, clumsily in her stockinged feet, her dress clinging so that the ridge of her girdle showed, her hair in wet drab locks. She went through the trees and across the lawn toward the terrace. Maggy started after her and then as Lydia seemed to need no help but only plowed on, Maggy ran back to the landing.

But nobody had seen Ralph. Nobody had thought of Ralph. She stood with Clare and looked and looked up and down the river and there was no swimming figure, no bobbing head anywhere.

"But he could swim!" Clare said. "It's practically the only thing he could do well. He *must* have got to shore somewhere! Kirk has gone to phone for the police launch."

But they waited, it seemed a long time, while the wide old Matoax took its even journey, dappling with sunlight, past them. Little eddies gurgled around the pilings of the old pier. Kirk came back. "The police launch is on its way. Anybody seen him?"

Clare shook her head. Alroy and Josh came struggling back through the heavy willows. "No sign of him anywhere," Alroy said. "Nothing we can do. I'm going to the house."

He looked exhausted; his big face was tinged with blue. They all trudged up the path to the house. Lydia was lying back in a long chair on the terrace and Emily was holding a cup of hot coffee for her. Emily didn't ask if they'd found Ralph; her pale, troubled eyes saw that they hadn't. "Dr. Mason is on his way," she said. "Maggy—I think Lydia has fainted."

Maggy stooped down over Lydia. Her eyes remained obstinately shut but her pulse was strong. As she leaned over Lydia she felt something put lightly over her bare shoulders; it was her dress, the full-skirted, entangling white dress she had dropped on the pier. For the first time she was aware of her short white slip which was wet and clung to her like her own skin. She looked up and Josh, beside her, said, "Keep that around you. No sense getting pneumonia."

Maggy huddled her dress around her. "Thanks, Josh." She turned to Emily. "I think this is just shock. She needs blankets, a hot-water bottle. Here, give me the coffee. Maybe I can get it down her."

"You go and get a hot bath and some dry clothes. You too, Clare. Josh, Kirk, let's get Lydia upstairs and into bed."

"Come on, Maggy," Clare said. "I don't know about you but my teeth are chattering."

That was shock, too, Maggy thought vaguely and went with Clare.

The long hot shower gradually checked a kind of exhausted tremor along her nerves; her dry clothing felt wonderful and normal. How could they have forgotten Ralph—missed him entirely—thought only of Kirk and Lydia!

It was strange and dreadful that somehow Ralph Hewitt was the kind of person one did forget.

She scrubbed her teeth, too; but all of them at one time or another in their childhood had certainly swallowed river water and no harm done. There were voices on the terrace.

She was fastening her fresh blue linen dress when she heard in the distance the swift chug of a powerful motor launch and went to the window. The sun was almost down now and that was good, for the softer light would make it easier for the police to search the river and the banks. The police launch, a big one and speedy, came into view and checked its speed just off the Beall landing. There were four men in it, two of them in swimming trunks. As she watched, the launch altered its course and started slowly to the opposite bank. Halfway across, it slowed down almost completely and one of the policemen poised himself for a moment and then dived into the river. After a few moments though he came swimming back to the launch so whatever they thought they had seen, it was not Ralph.

The launch zigzagged back and forth and then turned and headed downstream and out of sight around the curve, making now, she knew, for the bridge, two miles down, where the river narrowed between steep and rocky banks in a hurtling current.

She felt chilled again in spite of the heat of the day which lingered on in the big room. She turned toward the door and as she did someone knocked and Dr. Mason called to her. "Maggy?"

She opened the door and he came in. A kind of reassurance and warmth came in with him, exactly as it had done when she was a child and he had come to look at her throat or tell her mother that he really didn't think that she was going to have scarlet fever or anything. "Collywobbles," he would say and pull out the paper bag of fruit-flavored candies which always sagged down one of his pockets.

He did look older; he was tall, like Josh, but stooped; his hazel eyes were deeply pocketed in wrinkles but were keen and friendly; his once sandy hair was thick and brushy but almost white. He said, as he had always said, "Now let's take a look at you, young lady."

"How is Lydia?"

"Oh, she's all right. Strong as a horse. They've got her in bed in a room down the hall. Hold still now." He put his shabby leather bag on the table. "Left my stethoscope at the office but if I can't tell how anybody's heart ought to sound . . . Don't wriggle . . ." He held her with his firm, slightly gnarled and arthritic fingers while he put his white head against her chest. There was always about Dr. Mason a faint smell of antiseptics and tobacco. He lifted his head after a moment, put his hand around her wrist and gazed absently over her shoulder at the white cascade of the wedding dress while he counted. Then he said, "Nothing the matter with you. What's the idea, taking a swim when the Matoax is so high? Think you could pull Josh and Lydia and the whole batch of them out?"

"I guess I didn't think."

"Better think next time. Got any pills around—sedatives?"

"No."

"And you a nurse! Now stop looking like that, Maggy.

60

Ralph, why he swims like a fish. Nobody would think of trying to rescue him. If he's gone—well, it's an accident. Nobody could have helped it. If you can't sleep tonight . . . Here . . ." He opened his bag and took out a bottle full of red capsules. As he did so, Emily called from the hall, "Dr. Mason—somebody wants you on the phone."

"Oh Lord, I'll bet it's a country call and I was out all last night. See you, Maggy." He put the bottle down on a table and hurried out. He walked like Josh, too—or Josh walked like his father, taking long strides, intent on where he was going.

But Maggy felt better. It was an accident. Accidents happened.

She followed Dr. Mason into the hall. He was talking over a telephone extension which stood on a table down at the corner, where a narrow back corridor crossed the main hall. There was the vigorous sound of water running from behind one of the closed doors that lined the hall. She went down the stairs and out to the terrace. The beat of the police launch was clearer, as if it were coming back slowly, close to the shoreline.

Then she saw that George Clowe sat in a fat, loose huddle in one of the green chairs. His clothes, too, were sodden and dripping. He had a glass in his hand. His face was alarmingly splotched with red. He seemed to sense her presence and looked up with dull eyes.

"George!"

"They got her out, didn't they?"

"Lydia—yes! Dr. Mason is here. He says she is all right."

George stared at her blankly. "That's good—that's good . . ."

He sounded as if he'd been drinking too much; that or he was in a state of shock. But then they were all in a state of shock. She said, "George, you'd better get into some dry clothes," before the reason for his wet clothes struck her. "Why—you were in the river, too! I didn't see you."

"Heard her scream. Was getting into my car. Ran back around the kitchen—through the shrubbery . . ."

His hand was shaking so the drink in it splashed. She went to him and took the glass. He didn't resist; only watched her as she put it on the table. "Go upstairs, George. Get a hot bath and Kirk will lend you clothes."

"I didn't reach Lydia," he said suddenly. "Understand? I didn't get anywhere near her. Had to go back. I got scared and had to go back and she was drowning. I couldn't get there. . . ."

She went behind him, put her hands under his arms and hoisted him to his feet. "Come on now, George. You'll feel better."

"Got in the river—scared—it was awful. They got her out, didn't they?"

"Of course they got her out! She's upstairs in bed. She's safe."

He stood swaying soggily and he wouldn't move. The screened door on the terrace banged. Josh came across the terrace and at once understood the situation. "I'll take him." He put his arm around George, bracing him, and George shambled unevenly beside Josh, into the house.

Josh had changed clothes; he must be wearing clothes of Kirk's or Alroy's—slacks and a white shirt with no tie. His sandy hair was still wet.

It was a little cooler now. Evening shadows were growing long across the lawn and the terrace, with its bright gay chairs and the tray of glasses on the table. The red roses looked out of place, festive and untouched by tragedy.

It was queer that she hadn't seen George in the river. He must have run from the big circular driveway before the front door, on the east side of the house where he had left his car, past the kitchen end of the house and then plunged down through the shrubbery into the river. But she had been watching the commotion near the canoe; she wouldn't have seen anything else. George must have ventured only a little way out, as she had done, when he discovered the lethal strength of the current.

Josh came back, listened to the throb of the police launch, which was now returning, and said, "They are just about opposite the landing. Let's see if they have any news."

She went with him down the flagstone path to the landing. The police launch was as close inshore as it could come, just beyond the rocky shallows.

The men in the launch looked across at them. Josh shouted and although the men on the launch perhaps could not hear his question they knew what he asked, for one of them shook his head and another waved his bare arms in a gesture of negation. The launch went on slowly, turning again toward the opposite bank. The sunset had left a fiery rosy glow in the sky above the distant hills.

Josh said, "I'm afraid that's it. If I did think of Ralph, I only thought he might get to Lydia before I did. Honestly, though, I can't remember thinking about him at all. I just assumed he'd get out. . . . Maggy, you heard what Lydia said."

"Lydia . . ."

"She said, 'He tried to kill me.' Which one tried to kill her? Ralph? Or Kirk?"

SIX

Maggy looked at him with utter blank astonishment. "But that—what on earth do you mean?"

"Are you trying to tell me that you've forgotten what Lydia said?"

"Why, no, of course I remember it." She remembered, too, the blazing look Josh had given her, across Lydia, lying between them. So that was the significance of it. "I never even thought of it again!"

"A woman says that somebody tried to kill her and you never thought of it again?"

"I certainly didn't. Why, that's preposterous. It's childish. It's—people don't try to murder other people. . . ."

"Oh but they do," Josh said somberly, watching the police launch. "And I suppose that's how they get away with it sometimes. Just because it's hard to believe. There's a kind of barrier, a wall of disbelief. Murder is outside civilization. It goes back to the jungle. So we say, this person whom I know, with whom I've walked and talked, whose hand I've taken in friendship, cannot possibly be a murderer. Yet it happens."

"It didn't happen today. That's a dreadful thing to say!"

"What did you think that Lydia meant?"

"She didn't mean anything! She was flustered and scared. She had come very close to drowning. . . ."

"Yes, she did," Josh said soberly.

"Josh, listen to me. I didn't think anything of that. I really didn't, because she was so shocked and frightened. There are people whose first reaction when anything goes wrong is to blame someone else. It's almost automatic. If the—the dress isn't becoming it's the saleswoman's fault. If they miss a train it's because the taxi driver was slow."

"Did you think that when you heard Lydia say, 'He tried to kill me'?"

"I tell you I didn't think anything! Well . . ." she hesitated, seeking back to the moment below the willows. "I suppose I must have thought, she's scared and furious and taking it out on Ralph and Kirk because they were paddling and the canoe upset. Then they started looking for Ralph and—no. I never thought of it again because it didn't mean a thing."

He waited a moment before he said, "Suppose she meant exactly what she said."

"I tell you she didn't. Besides—why she couldn't have! There were only Ralph and Kirk in the canoe with her. Ralph Hewitt wouldn't hurt a fly. . . ."

"What about Kirk?" Josh said.

"Josh!" Anger welled up like a tide. "Let's have this clear. Yesterday you told me I mustn't marry Kirk. I thought you were only—well, never mind that. Now you as good as say Kirk tried to murder Lydia. That's simply not true and it's a frightful thing to say. What have you got against Kirk?"

He seemed to debate, watching the police launch with narrowed eyes. "Well," he said finally, "that's a fair question. I'll answer it fairly. I really have nothing against Kirk. But you can't marry him."

"You said that yesterday. Why?"

"Maggy." He turned to face her. "Postpone your wedding."

His face and voice were so grave that for a moment she was bewildered, as if she were groping in the dark, trying to find some signpost. "Do you mean—can you possibly mean because Lydia said that hysterical, stupid thing? Are you—why, are you seriously accusing Kirk of—of murder?"

"Attempted murder," he said soberly.

"Kirk! Why, you can't—I'll not let you—don't you realize what you are saying?"

"Oh yes, I realize it. I'm not accusing Kirk—or Ralph for that matter. But I'd like to know what happened in that canoe. . . ."

She broke in. "I'll tell you what happened. I know exactly. I was in my room, at the window. It's high enough so I can see over the trees. I saw the canoe come out from behind the trees. Lydia was facing the house. Ralph and Kirk were paddling. The sun was so bright I couldn't see very distinctly but I saw that. There was nothing wrong, nothing at all. I turned away from the window and then Lydia screamed and the canoe had upset. . . ."

"You didn't really see what happened at all then."

"I did see it. They were talking, I thought. Kirk seemed to turn a little and hold his paddle up in the air to speak to Ralph. Lydia didn't make a move. Nothing happened at all. . . ."

"But the canoe upset. Ralph, poor soul, is almost certainly drowned. Lydia nearly drowned—and then said, 'He tried to kill me'!"

"Josh, you've got to stop this. I mean it. It's not like you—it's wrong, it's horrible to talk of—of murder and Kirk and . . ."

66

He put his hands on her shoulders. There was something in his eyes that she could not understand. . . . Pain? Tenderness? His hands were gentle, yet so strong that she seemed to draw nearer him. "I'm sorry," he said. "Really, I'm sorry, Maggy. I have to . . ."

He stopped as the planks of the landing quivered. Kirk said, "Have they found Ralph?"

Josh's hand dropped. Maggy moved quickly away from him. But Kirk hadn't seen them—standing so close, Maggy thought, annoyed at herself. Kirk, too, was staring across the river toward the launch. They hadn't heard him approach; he was wearing rubber-soled moccasins.

Josh said, "No. They've been all along the opposite shore again."

With a half-defiant gesture she linked her arm through Kirk's. It was growing dark; the far reaches of the river were obscured in gray-blue shadows. Kirk said, "I never thought of Ralph. I only thought of Lydia—and of saving myself, I suppose. Self-preservation. I got hold of the canoe, I don't know how. I tried to push it toward Lydia. I remember that. But I couldn't; it was all I could do to hang onto the canoe. It happened so fast."

"How did it happen?" Josh asked.

Kirk thought for a moment. He too was freshly clothed in slacks and a light shirt; his crisp black hair was damp. He took cigarettes from a pocket, offered them to Josh and to Maggy and then held his lighter for both of them. "To tell you the truth," he said, "I don't know. It was so quick. Ralph and I were paddling and it struck me that we were getting too far from the bank. I hadn't realized that the current would be so strong. I said something about turning around and going back. Maybe that's what caused it—Ralph may have made some motion or misunderstood me or something. Canoes are tricky. Just all at once we started over and before I knew it, there we were in the water. I can't swim—I tried to make it to the canoe. Lydia can swim—but then I heard her screaming and I knew she'd lost her head. Ralph just disappeared. I thought he'd gone to help Lydia—if I thought anything. Then I saw you, here on the landing, and by that time I'd got a fairly good hold on the canoe. Thank God, you brought her out. I'd have never made it to her."

"Well," Josh said, "Alroy got there in time. I was just about exhausted."

"We saw you send Alroy to help Josh," Maggy said to Kirk. And that, she thought quickly, ought to answer Josh. Why hadn't she thought of it sooner? If Josh really thought that Lydia had accused Kirk of attempted murder, that argument alone should answer Josh. She said to Josh rather than to Kirk, "Kirk really saved both your lives, Josh—yours and Lydia's—sending Alroy to help you."

Kirk said, "Oh, no. Josh would have made it. I wasn't being heroic. I just knew by then that I could hang onto the canoe. You got there in a hurry, Josh. I was never so thankful for anything in my life as when I saw you running down to the landing."

"We didn't have far to come," Josh said. "We were in the garage looking at the new car you gave Maggy. We heard Lydia scream. We guessed what had happened."

"It was my fault," Kirk said. "I knew the river is high. We shouldn't have gone out in the canoe."

"I suppose Ralph suggested it," Josh said in an oddly toneless voice.

"Well, no," Kirk said. "I believe it was Lydia's suggestion. I didn't particularly want to go out in the river but —I really never thought of danger."

68

"That canoe has got air pockets, hasn't it?"

"Air . . ." Kirk looked a little surprised. "Why yes, I believe it has. It's aluminum. It has a small keel. Yes, of course, I'd forgotten. There are sealed-in air compartments at each end. We've had it a long time; Cousin Emily got it when Clare and I were children."

"Funny it upset like that. So suddenly," Josh said.

A little alarm bell seemed to ring somewhere along Maggy's nerves. In another moment, she thought, Josh would accuse Kirk of upsetting the canoe!

Kirk said, "All canoes upset at half a chance. This one is relatively safe. That's why Cousin Emily got it. but it happened."

Maggy said, "I saw it from my window. I was telling Josh. One minute the canoe was there and the next minute Lydia was screaming and—but I never once thought of Ralph."

Josh said, "None of us thought of Ralph. We were all to blame, Maggy."

"If it's anybody's fault it's mine," Kirk said. "I should have known. I should have stopped it. Or at least turned back sooner . . . Shall we go to the house? The police will phone if there's any news."

"The launch is still out there," Josh said, but they went back to the house, slowly along the flagstone path, past the bench and the tennis court and the red roses.

Emily and Clare were sitting on the terrace in a kind of listening, stunned silence. Alroy was standing at the balustrade, looking down toward the gleams of the river between the trees. Clare said as they came up on the terrace, "The police just phoned. They are afraid the body has drifted on down the river. They've posted policemen along the way."

Emily's hand went unsteadily to her lips. "They seem to think there's no hope."

"There's always hope, Cousin Emily," Kirk said gently.

Alroy gave a jerky laugh and came to stretch his big slack body on a long chair. "Don't tell her that, Kirk. We all know the old Matoax. Pretty as a picture and murderous as a tiger. What happened to George? He's up there on my bed, out like a light."

Josh replied, "He was here on the terrace. I got him upstairs. He kept mumbling about Lydia and the river. He must have tried to swim out to her and didn't make it."

"Yes, that's what he said." Maggy explained it briefly. Clare said thoughtfully, "That's queer. I didn't see him."

Emily looked at Josh. "Your father had a call to make. He said he hoped to be home to dinner."

"Thanks," Josh said. "I'll just phone—home if I may. . . ."

Emily nodded and he went into the house.

Emily said sadly, "Ralph was so proud of being a good swimmer."

"He got a cramp," Alroy said.

Emily sighed. "And just before the wedding." She seemed to struggle with some troublesome thought and finally said, "But of course it isn't as if he were a relative. Or even a close friend."

Clare instantly grasped the question behind it. "Certainly not! It's tragic. It's a dreadful thing to happen. But it was an accident. Everybody will understand. We can't possibly change anything about the wedding plans. There's no reason for it!"

"No," Emily said. "No, of course not. But I am so sorry it happened now. I wanted everything about the wedding to be perfect. . . ." Her voice wavered. Kirk went to her quickly.

"It *is* perfect," he said. "It *will* be perfect. I'd give anything if this hadn't happened but . . ." He took one of her hands and she looked up at him, her pale eyes asking for the reassurance he gave. "It's as Clare says, dear. It was an accident. I blame myself but nobody else could possibly have helped it. . . ."

"Kirk," Emily cried, "it wasn't your fault! You mustn't blame yourself. No—now we'll not talk about it." Her lips quivered a little, her eyes were steady. "We'll just not talk about it. We'll hope that he's safe somewhere. Why, I— I wouldn't think of changing anything about the wedding! I don't know whatever got into my head!"

Alroy struck a pose and said with burlesque drama, "The wedding must go on!"

It was a jarring, ugly note. Emily caught her breath sharply. "Alroy!"

Kirk's black eyebrows made a line across his white face. He said in a low voice, "Shut up, Alroy. You're drunk!"

But Clare was swiftly, shrilly angry. They were all strung to a high pitch, Maggy thought. Otherwise Alroy, even if he had had too much to drink, would never have spoken in just that jeering, ugly tone. Clare, however, flashed out at Kirk instead of Alroy. "Suppose he *is* drunk! He's got a right to be. If you hadn't taken out that canoe, nothing would have happened. *You* knew the river was high. Or you ought to have known it. *You* can't swim. Nobody ought to go out in a canoe if he can't swim. . . ."

"Clare," Emily cried, knotting her hands together again and leaning forward. "Please, Clare . . ."

And Maggy thought suddenly, where is Josh? He had had plenty of time to telephone.

Kirk went to Clare and put his arm around her. His white, angry look vanished; he smiled down at her with his own particular warmth and charm. "I'm sorry, Clare. We are all on edge."

Clare looked up at him defiantly, yet her face seemed to soften. Maggy slipped quietly behind Emily's chair and into the house. She knew exactly where Josh was and what he was doing.

Someone had turned on lights in the lower hall. From the dining room came the sound of servants' voices. Mildred said, "They'll never find him alive! Isn't it terrible, and just before the wedding!" Mrs. Elwell cut in sharply, "Get out those table mats. They'll have to use the small tables. We can't move all this stuff off the dining-room table."

Maggy went up the wide oak stairway. In the upper hall an open door gave her a glimpse of a shadowy room and George, full length on a bed. They must have put Lydia in one of the two or three small rooms around the corner of the hall. She turned the corner into the narrow crossing corridor. A door at the end of it was open. She heard Josh's voice. "Go on, Lydia. What happened?"

There was a kind of murmur from Lydia. Maggy came to the open door and stopped.

It was a small room. Lydia lay in the bed. The blankets had been flung in a tumbled heap at the foot of it. A sheet came up to her chin. Her light hair had partially dried and was still stringy and disheveled. Her lovely face was pale but somehow, sometime she had replaced the pink lipstick on her mouth so it looked curiously bright. Neither Josh nor Lydia saw Maggy.

Josh was sitting on the arm of a small chintz-covered chair, leaning over Lydia. His face looked pale, too, under its tan and as intent, Maggy thought again, as a hunter's.

He said, "*Go on, Lydia!* You said he tried to kill you. Tell me, Lydia, who?"

"Josh!" Maggy blazed with anger.

Josh didn't move, didn't even look at her. Neither did Lydia. She might not have been there. She ran into the room. "I knew you were here! I knew why!"

Josh made a little absent shrug as if he were brushing away a mosquito. He put his hand on Lydia's round white arm and shook it. "Tell me, Lydia. Who tried to kill you?"

Lydia's pale face looked slack; her dull eyes had tiny black pupils. Maggy cried, "Stop it, Josh! Your father gave her a sedative. You can't talk to her now."

But Lydia was going to talk. Her pink lips moved slowly. "I don't know what you are talking about."

"Lydia, listen—you said, when we got you up on the bank—you said, 'He tried to kill me.' Why did you say that?"

Lydia's eyes were fixed, yet something seemed to move behind that blank blue wall. She moistened her lips. Then she said clearly, "Nobody tried to kill me. I don't know what you mean."

"But you said . . ."

"*Josh,*" Maggy cried, "*stop it!*"

Lydia clutched the sheet around her and sat up, leaning on one elbow. "I said nothing of the kind. Nobody tried to kill me. It was an accident. It was an accident. . . ." She stared at Josh and then slowly settled back upon the pillows, jerked the sheet up to her firm chin and closed her eyes.

She wasn't going to talk again. That was as clear as if she had said it and there was something about her chin and her bright pink mouth that was convincing.

"All right," Josh said and stood. He looked down at Lydia for a second and then turned to Maggy, took her arm, and drew her out of the room and into the narrow corridor. He stood with his back to the window so his face was in the shadow. "You heard her say that!"

"I heard her deny it, too."

"Of course, she denied it. She's scared out of her wits."

"Scared . . ."

"She's afraid whoever tried to kill her today will try again."

"Get out of this house!" Maggy cried fiercely.

"Lydia was telling the truth the first time. And I'll prove it to you, you little fool!" Josh said with a strangely quiet deliberation and walked past her and out of sight around the corner of the hall.

SEVEN

She stood for a moment listening to his footsteps on the stairs, confused and shaken by waves of anger. He hadn't said Kirk, but he meant Kirk.

She would tell Kirk exactly what Josh had said, everything. He had a right to defend himself—but against what?

Against nothing. Against a few hysterical angry words of Lydia's. Against an inexplicable and ugly notion Josh had got obstinately into his head, which had no basis of fact.

Of course she wouldn't tell Kirk. She couldn't possibly hurt—and anger—Kirk, like that.

Besides—besides, it would mean an open and violent clash between Josh and Kirk.

No, it was better to keep the thing in its right proportion. Josh would eventually come to his senses. Yes and apologize, she thought angrily. Lydia called, "Come here. . . ."

She went back into the room and Lydia was sitting bolt upright. The sheet had fallen away and Maggy thought, with a little twinge of exasperation, that Lydia needn't have been so modest about the sheet for she was wearing a voluminous, high-necked nightgown of cambric, edged with lace. Lydia's eyes were glassy but full of purpose. "I've got to get out of here. Get me some clothes."

She didn't look as if she could walk across the room. Maggy said, "Did the doctor say you could go home?"

"That doesn't matter. I've got to go home. Get me some clothes."

"What did Dr. Mason give you?"

"I don't know. It doesn't matter. If you don't bring me some clothes I'll go like this!" Lydia glanced down at the nightgown and a kind of surprise diverted her. "Must be Miss Emily's," she mumbled. "Clare wouldn't wear anything like this. Hurry—get me a dress."

"All right," Maggy said, wearily. "Try getting up. If you can make it I'll help you dress."

"I don't need help. I'm not going to stay here." Lydia managed to prop herself up. She sat for a moment, her eyes and face completely blank. Then, without a word or even a sigh, she simply slumped back and closed her eyes.

That'll do for you, Maggy thought tersely, and pulled the sheet up over her. She glanced around the little room. A thermos and glass stood on a tray on the beside table. A black handbag stood on the dressing table—Lydia's, certainly, which explained her newly applied lipstick. Except for that and the tumbled bed with Lydia's figure making a flaccid hump below the sheet, the room looked unused and untenanted. Somebody obviously had taken Lydia's clothes away to have them dried, but Maggy opened the door of the little closet across the room, just the same. There were only empty hangers, some chintz-covered blanket boxes and a drifting, sharp odor of moth balls. So if Lydia awakened again and decided to dress and go home, she'd have to ask for clothes, and it would give them warning. Clearly, she wasn't in a condition to go home or anywhere and wouldn't be until morning.

Maggy went to the windows and pulled the shades

down. When she turned, she saw through the gloom in the room that Lydia wasn't asleep, not really; she was watching Maggy closely, her eyes like narrow blue slits.

Maggy went to the bed. There was one thing she was going to clear up. "Lydia—you *did* say that somebody— you said 'he' tried to kill you. Why?"

"I didn't. . . . At least if I did, I don't remember it. I was—shocked. Frightened. . . . Have they found Ralph?"

"No. Not yet."

"What happened to him?"

"Cramp, they think. Or the current was too strong even for Ralph."

Lydia looked at her blankly for a moment. Then she said, clearly, "He got hold of the life preserver—that kapok-filled cushion. I thought he was bringing it to me. But then I went down again and when I came up I couldn't see anything. . . . They'll never find Ralph."

"Go to sleep. I'll leave the door open. You can call if you want anything."

Lydia's eyes closed. After a moment Maggy went out of the room, quietly.

At the corner of the hall, though, she heard a kind of rustle from Lydia's room and stopped. The door behind her closed and a key rasped softly in the lock.

In spite of herself Maggy's heart gave a painful little thump.

"She's scared," Josh had said. "Afraid whoever tried to kill her today will try again."

That was preposterous! It was as horribly fantastic as the word, murder.

The only truly perplexing question was Josh, who was

as a rule level-headed and fair. Well, she couldn't account for Josh's vagaries and didn't intend to try.

She went on, past the open door to the bedroom on the left, and the room was now lighted. The bed was tumbled but George had gone.

Alroy or Kirk must have taken him home, that or he had roused and taken himself off. Poor George, she thought, blaming himself because he hadn't the strength he had expected of himself, he hadn't been able to fight that deadly current, he'd had to turn back. He must be still in love with Lydia, divorce or no divorce.

She went down the stairs again and out to the terrace.

She hoped that Josh had gone, and he had. Kirk was not on the terrace either and Clare and Emily were setting up two of the small folding tables which the caterer's truck had brought that morning. Alroy stood at the very end of the terrace, staring down toward the landing, and the glimpse of the river from there. There was again the chug of the police launch out on the river and now they had turned on a searchlight, which sent sweeping fingers of light across the trees.

Emily saw her. "Is Lydia all right?"

"Yes. She is asleep."

"I forgot to tell you. Dr. Mason told me to ask you to keep an eye on her tonight. He said he thought she'd be all right but there might be a little shock or something. . . ." Emily eyed her with a kind of surprise. "I keep forgetting that you were a nurse, dear."

It was not fully dark. There was a gentle twilight over the world although the shadows were heavy under the trees. However, Clare was lighting green glass hurricane lamps on the table, jerking at the matches and holding the tiny flames to the candles. She glanced up at Maggy over the flame of the candle she had lit and it touched her thin chin and high cheekbones with points of gold. "Kirk has been phoning the police barracks but there is still no news."

Emily took knives and forks from a tray and began to arrange them on the table. "Let's not talk about it," she said and counted the places. "Clare—we forgot George."

"Let's keep right on forgetting him," Clare snapped. "Except somebody has got to get him off Alroy's bed."

"No, he's gone," Maggy said. "I passed your room just now and he isn't there."

"Oh." Clare looked at her. "Well—that's one good thing."

Alroy came sauntering back from the end of the terrace. "Did you say George had gone? His car is still in the driveway, or was a few minutes ago."

"Oh dear." Emily sighed wearily. "You'd better make sure, Alroy. He is in no condition to be driving."

"Oh, he'll take care of himself," Alroy said lazily and was about to sink down into a chair when Clare snapped, "Do go, Alroy, and look."

"Well, all right." Alroy heaved himself reluctantly up again and started into the house as Kirk came out. "George has gone," he told Kirk. "Did you see him?"

"George? No. Are you sure?"

"I'm going to see if he took his car."

Kirk went with him. Mrs. Elwell came out with a casserole on a tray, put it down on the table and went back into the house, her crisp white apron whisking in the dusk.

"I think there's salad," Emily said, "and some sort of dessert."

"I'll get it," Clare said. "If we don't get rid of dinner before eight, she'll be off and we'll have the dishes to wash."

Maggy went into the house with Clare. As they gathered up a wooden bowl full of salad, plates of rolls and pie, Mrs. Elwell told them pointedly that it was nearly eight o'clock.

"Oh, all right," Clare said, "go ahead when it is time. You, too, Mildred. We'll see to the dishes. But make some coffee before you go."

Mrs. Elwell indicated that she would and looked at Maggy. "I am sorry about this," she said, "just before the wedding. . . ."

"It was an accident," Clare said sharply. "We are all sorry but it was an accident."

"There's ice cream in the freezer," Mrs. Elwell said.

Mildred looked at the kitchen clock and began to unfasten the pearl buttons of her white uniform.

"She can't wait to tell the whole village about it," Clare said in her clear and carrying voice as they went through the dining room.

"Mrs. Elwell?" Maggy asked, surprised.

"No, no, that girl Mildred. You've got to get some real servants in this house, Maggy."

"But I like Mrs. Elwell . . ." Maggy began. Mrs. Elwell had taught her own Sunday School class years ago with the same terse dignity and firmness with which she performed household chores for Emily.

"Nonsense. Cousin Emily got in the habit of economizing when Kirk and I were children and every penny counted. But there's money now. It's a big house and you will have to have parties and—no, you make Kirk get a good couple from New York just as soon as you get back from your trip." Holding the huge salad bowl in both hands, she backed against the screened door to the terrace and pushed it open.

It was a strange and unreal evening, dark, with clouds

that couldn't be seen but could be felt, pressing down close above them. The green hurricane lamps on the two tables cast waving gleams of light which seemed to distort and change the faces around the table. At one instant Emily seemed exactly like herself, a little worried but kind and placid, and the next instant the lines of worry deepened, there were pockets of shadow around her eyes, so she looked older and secretly troubled.

Clare's pale gray eyes reflected the lights and glimmered beneath her thick black eyelashes; she, too, seemed to change as the flames of the candles wavered, so her thin face was momentarily hard and anxious—and then she moved, the angle of the light revealing it different and softer. She smiled at Maggy and said in a matter-of-fact way that it was going to rain.

Alroy's big pale face, however, remained sullen and abstracted. Kirk was just as usual, the light striking upward and bringing his strong features and straight black eyebrows into prominence. Could Josh really believe that was the face of a murderer? She looked at Kirk across the table and he was watching her, his gray eyes clear, reflecting the gleams from the table. He smiled. "This time next week," he said, "we'll be in Paris."

"Yes," she said.

Alroy gobbled down pie and said between bites that it was odd about George. For George had simply, quietly disappeared.

Alroy and Kirk had gone to look for his car and it still stood in the driveway. They had taken a look through the house and George was not there. They had telephoned to the hotel where he was staying in Milbridge and he had not returned. They had even telephoned to the house he no longer shared with Lydia in Milrock and there was no answer. He hadn't changed to dry clothes or at least if he had, neither Alroy nor Kirk had discovered the clothes he would have discarded. The only explanation was that he had walked down the driveway in the same wet clothing in which he had dragged himself out of the river and thumbed a ride.

"He's in a bar somewhere," Clare said impatiently.

"That's not like George," Kirk said.

And all the time they listened—listened for the return of the police launch, and the police had given up for the night for it did not return to send its sweeping searchlights glancing along the bank. They listened for the telephone and a voice from police barracks saying that Ralph had been found but the telephone did not ring.

The candles made a green-tinged oasis of light which cast the rest of the terrace into deeper gloom. Clare and Maggy carried out the dishes and stacked them in the kitchen. "Mrs. Elwell won't like it," Clare said and shrugged her thin shoulders.

Emily wouldn't let them take the candles from the terrace. "No," she said with an odd urgency in her voice, leave them. . . ." It suggested Ralph might be stumbling up from some watery cove, needing a light to guide him.

"But nobody will need a light . . ." Clare began and checked herself. The candles remained in a green huddle on the balustrade after the folding tables had been returned to the library to join the other ranks of tables and chairs, and wait for the wedding and the reception which would overflow the house and grounds.

Alroy brought out a small radio and turned and turned through dance music, which sounded thin and far away as if it came from a distant but normal world, until he found a news broadcast. It was a local broadcast, from Milbridge.

Everyone listened intently, Clare as still as a cat at a mouse hole, Emily leaning forward so the lines showed sharply in her troubled face. After the national news the announcer said, "As to the local and state news. The Matoax, at almost flood stage, has apparently claimed another victim. This afternoon Ralph Hewitt of Milrock is presumed to have been drowned in an accident."

Alroy turned the radio louder. "At the home of Kirk Beall, rising young industrialist, president of the Beall Company of Milbridge—Ralph Hewitt, attorney of Milrock . . ."

It went on. The Matoax was very high owing to the snows of the previous winter and the prolonged spring rains. The canoe had overturned. Mrs. George Clowe of Milrock was rescued. Police had searched down river from Milrock as far as Berry Point. The body had not yet been recovered.

"Turn it off," Emily said suddenly and harshly.

"Now for the weather report." The announcer's voice brisked up. "Rain tonight—fair tomorrow—temperature . . ." Alroy snapped the switch. Emily said it was after eleven. "There is no use sitting up waiting," she told them firmly.

As the others went into the house, Kirk drew Maggy aside. "I'm sorry it happened. Try not to think about it."

"Yes, Kirk."

He took her in his arms and kissed her but that, too, seemed unreal, as if they were shadow figures. He sensed it, for he held her closer, his lips against her face. "You are the only woman who ever meant anything to me, Maggy. And you're mine. You know that, don't you?"

"Yes," she said. "Yes."

Before she snapped off the light at her bedside table she

83

looked again at her wedding dress, gleaming in its white folds of silk across the room. There was the light sound of rain on the terrace.

Gradually her tense nerves and weary muscles relaxed. Perhaps all of them were exhausted. Her last conscious thought was a curious one. Why, she thought suddenly, with the odd clarity of coming sleep, why had Lydia divorced George, who obviously was still in love with her, who still thought of himself as her husband and blamed himself bitterly for his failure to save Lydia's life?

It was no business of hers. She fell into sleep as if it were a deep and comforting haven.

She awoke with a start, feeling as if she were at the hospital on night duty, certain that she had some pressing and urgent responsibility. Why yes, Lydia! She had forgotten Lydia! Keep an eye on her, Dr. Mason had said.

It was very still. The rain had stopped. There was a faint dull glow coming from the windows which wasn't moonlight or starlight. For a moment or two she debated going to Lydia's room. Almost certainly Lydia was still sleeping heavily.

But the years of nursing discipline provided too strong and imperative a summons. She snapped on the bedside light, took her white dressing gown and slid her feet into slippers. But then she went to the window, drawn by the curious, tiny glow. When she looked down she saw that one of the green hurricane candles was still lighted, standing on the balustrade. It looked queerly lonely and out of place, shining in the night, its flame reflected on the wet and glistening foliage behind it.

They'd forgotten the candles, of course. Somehow this one candle had escaped the rain and was still burning.

She wrapped the dressing gown around her and quietly,

so as not to disturb the sleeping silent house, went into the hall. There was a dim night light in the corridor, near the stairs. All of the doors along it were closed and there was no sound anywhere. She went along the hall, down to the little crossing corridor. There was no light here so she felt her way along. She reached Lydia's door before she remembered that Lydia had locked it.

She tried the door, though, and it opened. Lydia must have regretted her impulse and unlocked it. The room was dark and very quiet. A moment passed before it struck her that the room was too quiet.

She took a step or two into the blackness toward the bed and stopped. All her senses told her that no one was in the room. No one lay there on the bed asleep. No one . . . But Lydia couldn't have crept out without clothes, left the house secretly in the darkness and the rain.

Her hand went out, hunted along the wall beside the open door, found the light switch and snapped it. The little room sprang into brightness.

She was wrong. Lydia was there, on the bed. Her face was turned down into the pillow. Her light hair looked dull.

And then something Maggy's trained senses had been trying to tell her emerged. She was at the side of the bed and did not know that she had moved. She couldn't see Lydia's face. She didn't have to see Lydia's face. She didn't have to seek and find Lydia's cold hand flung down over the side of the bed. Lydia was dead.

She couldn't be dead. Strong as a horse, Dr. Mason had said. Dr. Mason! That was the thing to do. That was always the thing for a nurse to do. Call the doctor. Call Dr. Mason.

She ran, stumbling in her high-heeled slippers, out of

the brightly lighted little room, along the narrow corridor, around the corner into the wide hall. The telephone stood on a little table. What was Dr. Mason's number? Oh yes, she remembered it. How many times had she called it! She dialed, her fingers jerking. There was a distant buzz as it rang. Josh said, "Hello . . ."

EIGHT

"Josh . . . I've got to talk to your father. . . ."

Instantly his voice became alert and sharp. "Maggy? What's wrong?"

"It's Lydia. She's dead."

"Lydia—*what?*"

"Your father—I want him to know. . . . He must come immediately."

Josh was fully awake now. "*What happened?*"

"I don't know. I—I went to her room just now. Dr. Mason said to keep an eye on her. And she—oh, Josh, get your father. . . ."

"I can't. He's on a country call—wait." There was a short pause. Then he said decisively, "I'll come right away. I've got a number—I'll call him. But I'll be there in a few minutes."

"Yes—yes . . ."

"Maggy." His voice was urgent. "Don't touch anything in the room. Don't wake anybody. Come down to the front door and wait for me. Understand?"

"Yes—no! No—I'd better call . . ."

"Don't call anybody. Do as I tell you. . . ."

The telephone clicked sharply. After a second or two the dial tone came on.

But she had to try to—well, suppose Lydia wasn't really dead!

She couldn't have made a mistake like that. But she went back, running lightly toward the bright light which poured from the open door of the little room.

Automatically she followed the rules which had been drilled into her. There was no pulse beat. She went to the other side of the bed; from there she could see a little of Lydia's face, dark in the shadow, and a glazed blue slit of one eye, half open and unwinking. There was not the faintest flicker of breath or life.

She didn't know, she wasn't experienced enough as a nurse to judge with any accuracy the time when Lydia had died. She was only perfectly sure that she was dead.

Dr. Mason had said that Lydia was strong as a horse. He had listened to her heart only that afternoon. Yet it had to be her heart, taxed beyond its strength in those terrified, struggling moments in the river.

She had died quietly. Perhaps she had never known that she was dying. The blanket still lay pushed down over the foot of the bed. The sheet was smooth. A pillow lay crumpled on the floor near the bed. So Lydia must have roused a little at some time, pushed one of the pillows away so that it fell to the floor and then drifted back into sleep again.

There were things she ought to do, chores that had been drilled into her. *Josh said not to touch anything in the room!*

Her mind leaped then as it felt the sharp sting of a whip. "Don't touch anything!" Was Josh going to say that Lydia had been murdered?

No, no! She almost said the word aloud. It then struck her that a long time had passed since she had telephoned to Dr. Mason and Josh had answered. Josh would be ringing the bell, pounding at the door, rousing the whole house. She had to get out of the room.

She was a nurse. She had seen death. It was true that she hadn't nursed for a long time and she had not acquired the kind of impersonal and professional viewpoint which a doctor or nurse must acquire. But she had never before been frightened.

She backed out of the room and gently, quietly closed the door.

She'd call Clare! But Josh would be arriving at any instant. She was halfway down the stairs, clinging to the bannister, feeling her way through her own shadow from the light in the hall above, before she remembered that she had intended to call Clare—pound at the door—open it and whisper—do anything, but anyhow call clear-headed, sensible Clare.

There was no light in the big hall below. It was like venturing into a strange place, and her own shadow tricked her; her hand struck the newel post before she expected it. Then she heard a car coming up the driveway. She felt for the last step, found it, fumbled her way to the front door and opened it. A car, with only parking lights turned on, coasted smoothly to a stop. The engine and the lights were turned off, the car door opened very quietly and Josh started toward the steps. She went running, stumbling in her high-heeled slippers, to meet him.

She reached the steps as he did and he put his arms around her. "There now—there now—stop shivering. . . ." He smoothed her tumbled hair with one hand and held her close in the curve of his arm, her head against his shoulder. "Don't be afraid. I'll see to things. . . . Tell me what happened."

"I went to her room. Your father said to keep an eye on her. It must have been her heart."

"Are you sure she's dead?"

"Yes! Oh, yes."

Scudding clouds cleared a little and for a second starlight shone down upon the graveled driveway and the black shrubbery; upon Josh's face, which looked in that clear starlight very white and set. Then the clouds swept across the entire sky again. Josh said, "I talked to my father. He said there was nothing he could do. He said you were a nurse, you wouldn't make a mistake. But he'll come as soon as he can."

"There is no chance—there's nothing anyone can do."

"You're cold. We'd better go into the house. Did you call anyone?"

"No. I was going to—I was going to call Clare—but I didn't."

"All right . . ." He led her into the hall. It was so dark that she could see only the dim path of light coming from the upper hall, barely outlining the bannister and stairs. Josh led her across the hall and into the living room. "Stay here," he said and found a chair in the dark, put her into it and turned back into the hall. For an instant his big body in khaki shirt and slacks loomed up dimly against the faint light and vanished.

He was going to call Kirk and Emily and tell them what had happened. "I'll see to things," he had said.

She was cold, and there was a chill sweep of air coming from somewhere. Then she saw that the door to the terrace was markedly lighter than the windows. The door was open.

Someone had forgotten that, too, as the hurricane candles had been forgotten. She rose, felt her way toward the door and stood there for a moment, looking out into the darkness. There was the sweet fragrance of honeysuckle. She remembered the faint, eerie glow of the forgotten hurricane candle but the terrace was now entirely dark, darker even than the other side of the house, for it was shadowed by the house itself and the heavy roses and wisteria and ivy. But the tiny green glow of the candle was gone, so it had at last burned out after clinging stubbornly to life during the rain which had drowned the other candles.

She could hear the slow murmur of the river and she thought of Ralph. Ralph—and now Lydia!

It was odd that there was no sound at all above, no voices, nothing.

She was wrong! Josh hadn't gone to rouse Emily, Kirk or anyone.

"Don't touch anything in the room!"

She must stop Josh!

She ran back through the living room and up the stairs. No one was in the upper hall, the doors were still closed. There was an air of sleep and utter quiet. If anyone had heard their voices whispering at the steps, if anyone had awakened, touched by a sense of uneasiness, there was no sign of it.

The door to Lydia's room was open and light streamed out. Josh was standing at the bedside table looking down. He heard her and swung around. "Shut the door," he said in a whisper.

She did, softly. He said, "Is this exactly the way you found her?"

"Yes."

"You didn't move her?"

"No, I—couldn't. But there was no use, Josh, there was nothing I could do."

"Her face was like that?"

"Down in the pillow like that? Yes."

"No, I mean was her face that color?"

"Color?" She looked at Lydia and quickly averted her gaze. "Why—why, yes."

"You don't understand me. Has her face changed color at all, since you found her? Come around here, Maggy."

She went around to the other side of the bed. She looked down again at Lydia; not quite half of her face was visible and it was a stony white. She saw the glazed blue slit between white eyelids and moved back swiftly around the bed, so she couldn't see it. "Yes—yes, of course. What do you mean?"

Josh was standing at the bedside table again. His hands were doubled up into hard fists and shoved in his pockets. "There was no real cyanosis?"

She stared at him. Josh was a doctor's son; he knew something of the vocabulary. A line in some textbook shot from memory: cyanosis is a blueness or discoloration—due to imperfectly oxygenated blood. "No!" she cried.

But she had a swift, chilling little memory. When she had run back to the room again after talking with Josh—hadn't Lydia's face seemed then dark in the shadow, tinged with a deeper kind of flush than now?

No, no, she told herself violently. That was merely the shadow.

But Josh saw the debate within her. "Are you sure?"

"You—you're saying . . ."

"There's a pillow on the floor. It's wrinkled, twisted. And—look here . . ."

She looked and didn't want to look, and could not avoid

seeing a pale pink smear on the wrinkled white pillow-case. "That's lipstick," Josh said.

"But she—she must have turned against it, she had on lipstick. That's nothing unusual. . . ."

"She was asleep. Drugged. It would be very easy simply to hold that pillow over her face until she died, wouldn't it?"

"Nobody did that," she whispered.

"It could have been done, and by now cyanosis would have disappeared. I know that much."

"You don't—it isn't true—it was her heart. . . ."

"That's only your guess, Maggy. Besides, all death in the end is heart failure. Did you see this?" From behind the thermos on the bedside table he drew a bottle, almost full of red capsules. "It's my father's. He carries this or one like it in his bag."

"But I—it was in my room. He was going to give me some capsules. Then Miss Emily called him and he went out and . . ."

"Did he put the bottle down?"

"I think—I think he put it on a table near the door but —that's all I remember."

"You haven't been in your room all the time since then. Anybody could have taken it."

She stared at the bottle with its bright red capsules and wished she didn't feel so cold and frightened.

"Look at the bottle, Josh! It's nearly full. There can't be more than a few capsules gone from it—not enough to . . ." Her voice was suddenly high and defiant. "She couldn't have taken—she couldn't have been given . . . If you're thinking *anything* it's not true."

"Of course I'm thinking something." His voice was low

and suddenly, savagely angry. "I should have stopped it. This is murder."

She didn't hear the door open. She only saw it move, quietly, out into the room. Kirk came in. He stood for a second, his face perfectly still and pale above his red dressing gown. His clear gray eyes touched her, went to Josh—saw Lydia. Without a word he went to stand at the bed and look down.

The little room was so quiet that Maggy could hear the low voice of the river. Then Kirk said, over his shoulder, "When did it happen?"

Josh replied, "Not long ago. Maggy found her like that. She called my father. He's on a call. I came." As he spoke he put his hand on Maggy's arm and drew her out, into the small corridor. Kirk followed them. Josh reached out and closed the bedroom door.

They stood together, in the small, dimly lighted corridor. It was still, yet Maggy felt as if currents of violence swirled around her, like the river, about to close over her.

Then Kirk said, "I heard you say this is murder."

"Yes," Josh said.

Their faces were in the shadow; their voices emerged in level, curiously polite tones. Kirk said, "You do realize what you are saying."

"Oh, yes," Josh said.

"But you—but Lydia . . ." Kirk stopped as a bell rang somewhere in the house. It rang again and again in short, imperative jabs. Josh said, "That's my father."

Kirk turned to Maggy. "You'd better go to your room, Maggy. Lydia wasn't murdered. I don't know what Josh is trying to do but whatever it is I'll put a stop to it."

His voice was still perfectly level. He smiled a little, reassuringly, but in the dim light his eyes looked icy, as if all the color had drained away from them.

The doorbell rang again, a long, demanding peal through the house.

Josh said, "I'll go and open the door."

"I'll go," Kirk said. "Murder! We'll see what he says to that!"

He went swiftly down the stairs; his red dressing gown, his black head disappeared into the hall below.

The hall itself lighted as he snapped on a switch.

Clare opened a door and stared at them. She clutched a bright green robe around her. Her black hair hung like a cloud to her shoulders. Her eyes were startlingly light and piercing between her heavy black eyelashes. She said, "Somebody's ringing. Who is it? *What's happened?*"

Down in the hall Kirk said, "Come in, Dr. Mason."

NINE

Maggy went with Dr. Mason back to Lydia's room; he ordered her to come; she was a nurse and she had found Lydia.

She watched him, alert to any doubt or question in his face; there was none. "Heart failure," he said.

Josh would tell him of the bottle of capsules. She pointed it out.

Dr. Mason lifted the bottle, gave it a close look and said, "I remembered this bottle as I was leaving, but it was an emergency call—man had been injured in a tractor accident so I didn't come back for it. I figured you're a nurse, you'd take care of it. Why didn't you?"

"I didn't think of it."

"Well—my fault. Probably Lydia came to your room, saw the bottle and took it. But I filled this bottle yesterday. . . ." He paused, as if counting, and shook his head. "She may have taken one or even two but I doubt it. Wouldn't have hurt her. I hadn't given her much sedation, just enough I thought to keep her quiet." He eyed Maggy. "I may be a country doctor, but I keep a pretty close check as a rule. . . ." He put the bottle of red capsules in his pocket. He pulled the sheet up over Lydia's face.

He led the way out of the room, and Josh and Kirk were waiting at the top of the stairs. Josh was leaning against the wall smoking; Kirk had one hand on the newel post. They were quiet and poised as two duelists waiting for their signal and Dr. Mason was the signal. Kirk said, "I want to talk to you, doctor. The others are downstairs. Will you come in here?"

They went into a narrow little room, once a sewing room apparently, for there was an old-fashioned sewing machine in one corner. A shabby couch stood against the wall, and a small rocking chair beside the one window. A bright light from the ceiling poured down. A dusty calendar dated June, 1950 hung crookedly on the wall above the couch. Maggy wondered where she had been in June, 1950 when the page of the calendar had been turned, and of course she had been in Milrock, counting the days at the Beall house as the big, exciting moments of her life.

Kirk said directly, "Josh says that Lydia was murdered."

Dr. Mason turned an utterly stunned and disbelieving face to Josh. "What on earth are you talking about?"

"Murder," Josh said. "Kirk told you."

Dr. Mason's eyes narrowed. His face tightened, his strong nose and chin jutted out fiercely. He shot one blazing glance at Maggy. "Shut the door. No use getting Miss Emily worked up. Now then—what's been going on here that I don't know anything about?"

Maggy closed the door. It struck her oddly that the small bare sewing room had changed subtly, in the fraction of a second. It was no longer simply a narrow little room, forgotten and unused; it was like a tiny courtroom with Dr. Mason the judge.

Kirk then was the prosecuting attorney; he directed the inquiry. He stood in the middle of the room with the bright light blazing down on his red robe wrapped tight

97

around him, his black head, his rather white and—Maggy saw then—angry face. He was quiet, he was in command, but he was angry; his eyes were very still but very light and bright between their extravagantly black eyelashes. He was frowning; his nose was pinched with anger.

Josh lounged across to the little sewing rocker and sat down; it was too small for him, his long legs stretched out. He still had a cigarette in his hand and he looked as if he had all the time in the world to make whatever statement he intended to make.

Dr. Mason sat down, too, wearily, on the shabby old couch which creaked. His voice was stern. "I asked you a question, Josh."

Josh squinted at the toes of the floppy old moccasins he wore. "Her face was down into the pillow. You saw that. You had taken a look at her late in the afternoon—obviously, you thought she was all right then, nothing wrong with her. Maggy found her about half an hour ago. There was at that time a slight shadow on her face which may have been cyanosis. . . ."

"Cyanosis . . ." Kirk repeated.

"A deep flush," Josh replied, still squinting at the toes of his moccasins. "Comes from lack of oxygen. Grows less and soon disappears—unless of course it is caused by gas poisoning. A pillow lay on the floor. There were lipstick stains on the pillow. If Lydia had been smothered the cyanosis would have disappeared—had disappeared fully by the time you got here, Dad."

He looked at his cigarette, meditatively.

There was a little silence. Then Kirk said, "And is *that* why you said murder?"

Josh nodded once.

But that was not the reason, at least it was not the whole

reason. Maggy did not even debate her course; the word *murder* was out, it was like a gate swung open, giving a glimpse of a forbidden country, peopled by dim, unnatural shapes—so the gate had to be swung back again, closed and bolted. She would not tell Kirk or anyone that Josh had all but accused Kirk of murder; no, she wouldn't do that. But she began, "Josh said—that is, Lydia said . . ."

And Josh said loudly, over her own voice, "That's enough, isn't it?"

He didn't look at her. Neither Kirk nor Dr. Mason seemed to note Josh's swift interruption.

Dr. Mason said slowly, "I didn't see any evidence of cyanosis."

"You wouldn't by now, would you?" Josh asked.

"Well—it depends." Dr. Mason looked at Maggy and she wished she were downstairs with Emily and Clare, she wished she were anywhere but in the narrow, bare little room with the light blazing down and the feeling that it was a courtroom debating life and death—debating murder. "What about this, Maggy? Did you note any cyanosis?"

Had she or hadn't she?

The room was very still, too still; she wished somebody would move or speak. She wished Josh would put the cigarette he held in an arrested, waiting way, to his lips. She wished Kirk would come to her rescue and say, how could Maggy possibly have noticed something that wasn't there? Or was it there?

It was a courtroom and she was the witness and she saw then that everything depended upon her answer. There was no murder, no case to be tried, without her testimony. She had to reply. "There may have been a sort of shadow from the light—I mean her face was in the shadow. . . ."

"Well," Dr. Mason demanded testily, "was it cyanosis or wasn't it?"

She swallowed hard and forced herself to meet Dr. Mason's piercing, angry eyes. "I'm not sure. I didn't think of it. The light was so bright and her face was turned away. Of course it was in the shadow and—I was upset and—and upset . . ." She thought fantastically, a real prosecuting attorney could make hay of that; he'd turn it and twist it, he could make anything of it, even a flat outright accusation of murder.

"Great God in the morning!" Dr. Mason shouted with such shattering force that Maggy jumped. "You call yourself a nurse!" He surged up from the couch and flung the door open. His footsteps thumped down the hall toward Lydia's room.

I should know; I should be able to answer, Maggy thought miserably. The heartening fragrance of coffee being made downstairs filled the room, and in its homely everyday fact denied murder.

Dr. Mason came back and then, flatly and certainly, denied it, too. He stopped at the telephone and dialed; they could hear him speak. "Thompson? This is Dr. Mason. Sorry to get you out at this hour. It's Mrs. George Clowe. Died of heart failure just now. . . . No, she's at the Beall place in Milrock. . . . Right away? Good. I saw her this afternoon. There was a canoe accident—oh, you heard about it. . . . Death certificate—oh, certainly. . . . Right, thanks."

He came back into the sewing room. He was still angry, mopping his face with quick jerks of the handkerchief. "Now then—I was surprised to hear that Lydia died, I'll not deny that. I didn't have my stethoscope with me this

100

afternoon, that's true, too. Certainly I did not detect any-thing that would have justified, say, sending Lydia to a hospital or getting in a heart man. But in all probability nothing in the world could have been done to avert this. The human body is a complex machine, in many ways still a mysterious machine. Accidents happen. I've lived and practiced medicine"—he gave Josh a fiery glance—"for many years. I ought not to be surprised at anything. My opinion is that there was an unsuspected heart weak-ness, an almost undetectable one. I am too experienced to believe that I could have missed anything overt. But there was consequently a delayed shock and death. If I had any doubts at all it would be my duty to report them to the coroner and suggest an autopsy. I have no doubts. If George isn't satisfied, if he wants an autopsy, he'll have to give me permission . . ."

"They're divorced," Josh said.

His father darted him a surprised look. "I hadn't heard that! When? Why?"

Kirk said, "Nobody knew about it but George."

"H'm. Well, that's George's business. The point is he'll know what to do, arrangements and all that. I've signed the death certificate. Now then, Josh, you have made a very serious accusation. I expect you to retract it."

Kirk said quickly, "Now wait a minute, doctor. Josh said that a suspicion of—whatever you call it—cyanosis was the reason he suggested that Lydia was murdered. But Josh is surely too sensible a man to make so serious an ac-cusation on such a slight and doubtful basis. What's the real reason, Josh?"

"I told you. That's enough, isn't it?" Josh said and again didn't look at Maggy, yet he might as well have com-manded her not to tell what she was going to tell. But she intended to have it out, nail it for what it was, and close that dreadful gate forever.

She said, "I can tell you the real reason. When they got Lydia out of the river she said, 'He tried to kill me.' Josh and I heard her."

Josh's face didn't change, not really—there was only a faintly tighter look around his mouth. But he hadn't wanted her to tell that.

Kirk stared at Maggy and then at Josh. "Is *that* the reason for all this talk of murder?"

Josh said, "Naturally I—remembered it."

Kirk said, "But—what did she mean? Who tried to kill her?"

Maggy said hurriedly, "She denied it later. Josh went up to her room and questioned her. He asked her who had tried to kill her. She said that she hadn't said anything of the kind. She said nobody tried to kill her. She was upset, she didn't know what she was saying, she was frightened."

Kirk said to Josh, "You questioned Lydia!"

Josh nodded again.

Kirk said slowly, "I was in the canoe—Ralph was in the canoe. You and Alroy rescued her. Who could have tried to kill her?"

Josh shook his head and finally spoke. "It's as Maggy told you. She denied saying it at all."

"But look here, Josh, if you believed her at first, even if you had any question, any doubt at all," Kirk said, "why didn't you do something about it?"

"What?" Josh said.

"Why, tell us about it. Give us a chance to—oh, be on the lookout, try to protect her."

"Would you have believed me? When Lydia herself denied it?"

"No," Kirk said candidly. "Nobody would have taken it seriously."

Maggy said unexpectedly, "Lydia locked the door of her room."

All three men swerved around to look at her. She said, "After I left her this afternoon, I mean after Josh had questioned her. She said she was going home and wanted some clothes. But then she saw that she couldn't so she went to sleep—that is, she pretended to go to sleep and as soon as I'd gone she locked the door. I heard it."

There was a rather long silence which seemed nevertheless packed with speculation. Finally Josh said, "How did you get into her room tonight, then?"

"I forgot she'd locked the door. When I tried it, it opened."

There was another lengthy silence. This time Dr. Mason answered the obvious question. "She unlocked it herself, of course. Probably decided she was going home—got as far as your room, Maggy, where she got those capsules. . . ." He caught a questioning movement of Kirk's and explained briefly. "Bottle of sleeping capsules in Lydia's room, taken from Maggy's room. Lydia may have taken one or two of them, but I don't think she took any and it wouldn't have hurt her if she had. Point is, Lydia herself unlocked that door. If she wanted to lock it or unlock it, what difference does it make! Good heavens, if she'd been afraid—if she'd really meant that somebody tried to kill her, she'd have told somebody—told everybody, called the police, shouted it from the housetops!"

His anger exploded again, this time at Josh. "And you have tried to stir up a mare's-nest because of some fool thing a woman yapped about—a woman just rescued from drowning, didn't know what she was saying. She could have blamed anybody for upsetting the canoe! She denied meaning anything else. Attempted murder! Now then, I want to hear you apologize!"

Kirk interposed, "No, no. Josh was right. I can see that he had to clear this thing up. So did I."

"He can mind his own business," Dr. Mason snorted, started for the stairs and turned back. "Now, not a word more of this, Josh. Understand? I don't want Miss Emily or—good heavens, the whole town of Milrock . . ." A puzzled look struggled with the anger in his face. "This isn't like you, Josh. What's the matter with you?"

"You've said it wasn't murder, Dad. All right. That should settle it."

"That's a retraction. It's not an apology!" Dr. Mason snapped.

"But Josh needn't apologize," Kirk began. "He was right to clear it up. . . ."

Dr. Mason didn't hear; he was storming down the stairs. Josh said mildly, "He's tired. Hasn't had much sleep for two nights. I'd better go with him."

"Wait a minute, Josh." Kirk's face lit up with warmth and candor. "I don't know just how to say this. But I think I know what's wrong. It's Maggy, isn't it?"

Josh lifted a startled eyebrow. "Maggy?"

"I know you're very fond of Maggy—always have been, I expect. Now that she's going to marry somebody else—me—well, hasn't it struck you that you want her yourself?"

Josh's startled eyebrow was still lifted. "You mean that I said it was murder in the hope of putting off the wedding?" he said directly. "Start an investigation, make trouble, put a spoke in the wheels. Is that it?"

"Oh, no! At least not intentionally. You wouldn't plan

it deliberately. Perhaps not even consciously. But you can't help knowing that any investigation into possible murder might . . ." Kirk shrugged and put out his hand in a swift gesture of friendliness. "All's fair in love and war, is that it?"

Josh eyed Kirk thoughtfully. Unexpectedly then he took a quarter from his pocket, looked at it and flipped it into the air. It fell with a little clunk onto the old sewing machine. Josh bent over it, looked at it minutely again, and thrust it back into his pocket.

Kirk drew back his hand. A tiny wrinkle came between his eyebrows. "Don't play games, Josh."

"Oh, I'm not playing games." He faced Kirk with an odd, rather rueful gleam in his hazel eyes. "The fact is you may be right about me—and Maggy. Good night, Maggy," he said pleasantly, walked out of the room and down the stairs.

His tread was light and quick. Maggy listened and Kirk listened. When the front door opened and then closed, Kirk turned to Maggy. "Poor old Josh! I'm sorry about all this, Maggy. I think from the first moment I saw Josh, there at the arbor yesterday, I knew something was different between us, something was wrong. He'll get over it. If he didn't know that he wanted you until you're as good as married to me," Kirk said good-naturedly, "then he's not going to die of love. He wouldn't really have tried to make trouble deliberately. I'm sure he wouldn't have done that. Probably he didn't realize that that was his motive. Well, he's not the first man to decide he's in love with a girl just as she's to be married to another man. But he's not a dog in the manger, not really. He'll not make any more trouble, Maggy."

But he's not in love with me at all, Maggy thought indignantly. And then she thought with utter cold conviction, he *is* going to make more trouble. "You're too reasonable, Kirk. Too fair. Too generous. You make excuses for Josh."

"That's easy. I can afford to be magnanimous. I'm getting the girl."

He stood, his hands in the pockets of his red robe, the light shining down upon his half-smiling, half-thoughtful face and crisp black hair with its touches of white. The fairy prince, Maggy thought, generous and fair, understanding and forbearing—why, I'm more in love with him than ever.

He wouldn't have been so generous if he had known that Josh had implied—no, he had more than implied it; he had all but accused Kirk outright of attempted murder. "Which one of them was it—Ralph or Kirk. . . ."

And Kirk wouldn't have been so generous if he had known that Josh flatly, strongly, opposed their marriage. "You can't marry Kirk—he's not the man for you."

Kirk said, "I'm trying to think why Lydia would say just that. You heard it. What do you think?"

"I don't think she meant anything. She said so later when Josh questioned her. She was hysterical, Kirk, she was upset. . . ."

The tiny wrinkle appeared between his black eyebrows again. "She'd have been thoroughly scared, of course, and then as soon as she got her senses she might have been just as thoroughly furious. Taking it out on anybody, blaming me or Ralph or—anybody."

"Josh had to knock her out," Maggy said. "She could have been thinking of that."

He considered it and shook his head. "I think she'd understand that. Josh certainly wasn't trying to kill her—

Lydia couldn't have thought even for a moment that Josh was trying to kill her. Or Alroy. Why, Alroy couldn't have—oh, tried to keep her face under the water at the very time he was helping Josh rescue her. You'd have seen that. Besides—oh, it's preposterous. . . ." The line, though, deepened between his eyebrows. He looked at her fully, his gray eyes as clear and sparkling as water. "Maggy, you said that you saw the whole thing, the canoe accident, from your window. Was there anything the least bit—oh, suspicious, unusual? I know that there wasn't another boat around, I'd have seen that. But did you see exactly what happened?"

"Yes," Maggy said and stopped, because all at once the sewing room became a courtroom again, the bright light as sharply inquisitive as a floodlight. Again her reply could establish or demolish any charge of murder. So she must be very careful and truthful. She said slowly, "That is, I was standing at the window of my room when the canoe came out from beyond the trees—so I could see it, I mean." She was frowning, trying with all her will to dredge up every small detail of that flashing picture. "Lydia was sitting, she was facing the house. She looked— oh, composed, sitting up very straight. Ralph was at the other end of the canoe, his back was turned to me. He had a paddle in his hand. You had a paddle, too. You lifted it and turned a little as if you were saying something to Ralph or he had said something to you. Anyway—well, that's all. I had just turned away when Lydia screamed. The canoe had capsized. I didn't see it go over. There was —oh, it was hard to see, the sun was so bright. . . . I ran downstairs."

Kirk was staring thoughtfully at the floor, seeming to survey the picture she had presented. And Maggy saw, with a kind of cold dismay, that what she said now made an incomplete and indecisive picture. It was exactly the way she had replied to Dr. Mason's question as to whether or not there were traces of cyanosis in Lydia's face. Why couldn't she give a flat yes or a flat no? Again, a prosecuting attorney or any lawyer skilled in courtroom tactics could make hay of both replies, could twist and turn either one to make it sound exactly as he wanted it to sound—not so much evidence of murder, but certainly failure to prove conclusively, beyond the shadow of a doubt, that it was not murder.

Kirk said, "Did Ralph make any sort of—oh, abrupt move? Anything like that?"

I didn't see it. I don't know."

"You see, I had a feeling that he *had* made some sort of move. I remember turning around to say we'd better go back. Just as I put my paddle in the water again there was a sort of jolt, a swerve—almost as if Ralph had moved suddenly, stood—I don't know what. It happened so fast. . . . But I can't see any reason for Ralph trying to upset the canoe. Certainly not to drown me, because that is what it would amount to, you know—I mean if there were a question of an intentional, contrived sort of accident. Ralph was an expert swimmer. I can hardly swim a stroke. To tell you the truth"—he gave her a half-ashamed smile —"I think I'm afraid of water. Lydia could swim but she wasn't like Ralph. She could keep afloat, but I suppose in that current—well, she lost her head and got in a panic. You're sure you didn't see Ralph get up in the canoe or make any sort of sudden move?"

"No," Maggy said, "I told you—I had moved away from the window just as you turned around to speak to

Ralph. I was going to go downstairs. Then I heard Lydia scream."

It was not a clear eye-witness account at all. It was just as wishy-washy, just as capable of being turned this way and that, as her reply about Lydia and a possible lingering cyanosis had been. She sighed and Kirk heard it. He turned to her. "Darling," he said, and she went into his arms as if she were magnetized. She pressed her face against the smooth silk of his sleeve.

"It was an accident," Kirk said. "Josh is the only one who ever thought of anything else, and we both know— at least, I know—why Josh brought up such a preposterous question. All the same, since he did bring it up, it had to be answered. Now forget it." He put his hand around her face and turned it upward. His lips brushed her mouth and then returned, full and urgent, upon her own. The half-frightened, half-shy tingle came at once, swiftly. At the same time, as always, she felt for the flicker of a pulse beat that this man holding her so closely, his mouth hard and seeking upon her own, this man whom she had known all her life, was a stranger. She pressed closer, seeking reassurance, and in the same fraction of a second contrarily she drew back a little.

Her withdrawal offended Kirk. She saw the tiny line between his eyebrows. Oddly, she was beginning to dread that faint small line. But then, before she could explain or apologize or say, stammering, I don't know why I did that—I love you so much, I love you even more than I did before—Kirk, generous, wise Kirk understood. The tiny line vanished. He put his hand gently on her face, on her throat. "It's like silk," he said. "Still a little shy, aren't you, darling? But I can feel your pulse—it's beating just

109

here. . . ." His fingers sought out what was, Maggy knew, a wildly thudding rhythm.

Someone in the corridor outside coughed and seemed to try to smother it. Kirk said, surprised, "Who's that?" and went to the door and jerked it open. "Alroy!"

Alroy came into view; he wore a white terrycloth robe which made him look enormous. His slaty eyes swept Maggy curiously. Surely he hadn't been listening to all that talk of murder, she thought. He had been; she was suddenly sure of it. Dr. Mason had shouted—Josh, Kirk, none of them, had bothered to lower their voices. Where could Alroy have been standing so he was out of sight? Why yes, there was the corner of the hall which led to the back stairs.

Alroy said, "I can't find George."

"Did you try the hotel in Milbridge?"

Alroy nodded. "His room doesn't answer. I phoned to his house—I mean Lydia's—anyway, their house. No answer there, either."

"He's sleeping off his drunk, I suppose. He must be at one place or the other. Get on your clothes and take your car and find him."

"I'm no errand boy," Alroy said unexpectedly and clutched his white robe defiantly around him.

Oh, don't, Maggy thought, don't try Kirk too far! He's given you a job, he's given you a home, he's done everything for you. Don't try him too far!

But Kirk's voice was as cold and clear as ice water. "Someone has to find him. Arrangements have to be made —Lydia's relatives, if she had any, have to be notified."

Alroy cut in. "George has no authority. Not any longer."

"But he'll know what to do," Kirk said patiently.

110

There was a moment's silence. Then Alroy's eyes· flickered and lowered.

"Oh, all right, I'll go," he said sullenly and went down the hall slowly, as if to emphasize his reluctance.

Maggy closed her eyes. Tomorrow, she thought, tomorrow we'll be away from all of it—Alroy and his sullen, slaty eyes, Lydia and George, and a dreadful, shocking accident which was only an accident but dreadful just the same. She would be married to Kirk and on the plane, safely winging along through the night.

Kirk said quietly over his shoulder, "You said I made excuses. But Alroy rather liked Lydia, you know. It's been a shock to him."

The doorbell rang. It was a long, very decorous peal, as if whoever rang did so with the most dignified solemnity possible. Kirk went to answer it.

TEN

The tread of the men up the stairs, along the hall and almost immediately down the stairs again, was decorous, too. Even the departure of the car was measured and slow, as if its very engine had been trained to express respectful sympathy. Another car backed out of the garage and shot past the car from Thompson's Funeral Parlor, its lights glancing against the bank of laurels; it was Alroy, on his way to find George.

When both cars had disappeared, Maggy left the window of the sewing room. There were voices from downstairs. Emily and Kirk were talking in low, subdued tones. Clare came up the stairs, a glass in her hand. "I brought you some hot milk," she told Maggy. "Cousin Emily said to see to it that you get some sleep."

Clare led the way to the big guest room; she gave Maggy the steaming glass. But then she sat on the foot of the bed, shoved back the masses of her black hair and said, "Alroy said that there was some talk of just how Lydia died. He was in the hall and overheard a little of it. What was it?"

Maggy leaned back wearily against the pillows and sipped the milk. The plain truth was the simplest answer; on the other hand, there was no use in, as Dr. Mason had put it, stirring up a mare's-nest. "There was an idea that Lydia might have got a pillow over her face and suffocated. Dr. Mason said that wasn't so, it was heart strain and shock."

Clare, though, was like Kirk; she picked things out of the air. "Who was supposed to put the pillow over her face?"

"Nobody did. I told you. It was heart strain."

"Well—whose idea was it that it might have been murder?"

Trust Clare not to mince matters, either. She said the word *murder* without flinching. On the other hand, her eyes were so drained of color between those extravagant black eyelashes that they were as pale as a frozen brook between black and wintry rushes.

Maggy replied, "Her death was unexpected. It was best to make sure that the cause of it was clearly established. Just so there wouldn't be any question later."

Clare thought that over, her pale eyes watching Maggy. "Are they going to do an autopsy?"

"Dr. Mason said no. There was no need for it. Unless, of course, George or someone of her family wants it."

"Kirk said that you found Lydia. You phoned for the doctor. He said the doctor was out on a call and Josh came. Why didn't you call some of us?"

"I intended to call you," Maggy said truthfully. "Then I knew Josh would be arriving, and he had said to open the front door for him. I was halfway down the stairs before I remembered that I was going to call you." And that had been rather odd, Maggy thought absently, obeying Josh's orders as if she were compelled to obey.

Clare said thoughtfully, but accepting it, "Of course, it was a shock to you. Was it your suggestion or Josh's that Lydia might have been murdered?"

"Clare!" Maggy sat up. "She wasn't murdered. Dr. Mason said so."

"Then it must have been Josh who talked about murder. Why?"

Maggy felt as if she were in the courtroom again, this time being cross-questioned. She sipped more milk to give herself time and wished that Clare would go away. Clare said suddenly, "If somebody is murdered, somebody else has got to murder her. Did Josh think one of us walked in there and put a pillow over Lydia's head?"

"I told you. Dr. Mason said that nothing like that happened."

Clare got up with a swoop of her green filmy robe and reached for a cigarette. "Don't be cross. I was thinking of George. I mean—well, I wonder where he's been all night."

This time it was Maggy who picked up the implication. "George wouldn't have murdered her! He's still in love with her! Isn't he?"

Clare went over to the window. "I didn't say he murdered her. Yes, he certainly behaved this afternoon as if he were still in love with Lydia." She paused and amended that. "Yesterday afternoon, that is; it's nearly two-thirty."

"Clare—why were they divorced?" She didn't know exactly why she asked it, but it seemed important.

Clare's thin shoulders shrugged. "Another man."

"*Who?*"

"Oh, that's always the reason for a divorce, isn't it? Another man, another woman."

"Well, but—I don't think that can always be the reason."

"It is always the reason," Clare said definitely. "A lawyer told me that one time. That is, it may not be a specific other man. He meant, I suppose, that there is the idea of another man, another marriage. He said that a woman isn't at all likely to give up a home and support and the married woman's status unless she believes in her heart that she can walk into another marriage. And usually pretty promptly."

"That's cynical, isn't it?"

"Maybe. Lydia had a well-developed sense of preservation."

"But all of Milrock would have known it if there had been another man."

"No, I don't think so," Clare said slowly. "Not with Lydia. She was propriety itself. At least outwardly. I've always suspected that if Lydia decided she wanted anything she wouldn't stop at any means to get it. But she was so proper it hurt. She'd have died before she started the slightest whisper of talk."

She did die, Maggy thought, and felt a long shiver start in her body. She finished the hot milk and put down the glass. Clare said, "If Lydia had another man in view, she'd have managed it so discreetly, so secretly—probably keeping him at arm's length, as a matter of fact, until she got herself divorced and all set for another marriage—that nobody, even nobody in Milrock, would have known it." She didn't look at Maggy, but she said, "You're shocked. I didn't like Lydia. No use pretending I did."

But Alroy liked her, Maggy thought. And then thought, could Clare possibly suspect that Alroy was the man who was the cause of Lydia's divorce?

A new and frightening thought leaped into her mind; Clare had instantly thought of George. So then had it occurred to Clare, because of the talk of murder, that

George had been jealous of Alroy and had actually come back and, from jealousy, murdered Lydia?

But it wasn't murder.

Clare said unexpectedly, "Ralph wasn't Lydia's lawyer. About the divorce, I mean."

Maggy sat up against the pillows. "How did you know that?"

"I asked him," Clare said coolly. "I intended to ask him why she got a divorce—I knew I could get it out of Ralph. But he said he believed that she had some lawyer in Puerto Rico. That's where she got the divorce."

"When did you ask him that?" Maggy asked in astonishment.

"Yesterday afternoon. On the terrace, just as we were starting down to the tennis court. There wasn't time to ask him anything more," Clare said rather regretfully.

And she had followed the course of reasoning which had leaped into Maggy's mind, for she said slowly, "But I don't think Lydia would have told George—about any other man, I mean. No, I think she'd have put it on a very high plane. Ideals—self-fulfillment—darling George, our marriage was a mistake. But let's not quarrel, let's remain friends. Meantime, be sure to send the alimony checks."

"You don't know that!"

"I knew her," Clare said, and turned from the black-screened window. She went over to Maggy's wedding dress and looked at it. "I didn't wear a wedding dress. I told you. I eloped."

"Why?" Maggy asked irresistibly.

"Because I was in love with Alroy and I snatched him before he could change his mind," Clare said, with an astonishing effect of simple truth.

"He wouldn't have changed his mind!"

116

"I wasn't sure. I wasn't sure of anything except I wanted to marry Alroy and I wanted to live my own life. So I married him and in six months I was right back here again."

"But this big house is here. Only Kirk and Cousin Emily —they wanted you. You have an interest—a big interest —in the works. Alroy's job . . ."

"Oh yes, all very rosy. Except it isn't." Clare picked up a fold of the white silk and examined it minutely. "Maggy, you are in love with Kirk, aren't you?"

"Yes!"

"I thought so. I'm going to tell you the truth. I like you and I want you to marry Kirk. But one reason I'm so keen on this wedding is because I want to get out of this house. Up to now, you see—as you pointed out—it's been so logical, so reasonable, for me and Alroy to live here that we just couldn't leave. Now it'll be different."

"You want your own home, of course."

Clare laughed shortly. "I don't give a hoot for my little love nest with Alroy. The point is, things haven't been —it just hasn't worked, that's all," Clare said a little desperately, letting the fold of white silk drop. "It's not been good for Alroy and it's not been good for me. Alroy . . ." She paused, looking at the white silk with those pale eyes behind which her thoughts darted so accurately and swiftly. "Alroy resents Kirk. You must have seen that. Kirk is smarter than Alroy. But the resentment carries over to me a little. I think once you are married to Kirk, and Alroy and I get away from here—oh, I think things may be better. And I'll have my piano."

She wouldn't accuse Alroy of having been attracted to other women (or to Lydia?) even if it happened to be the truth. Maggy fumbled for something to say that would

117

steer the talk from Alroy, and caught the word *piano* as if it might be a cue. "Your music . . ."

Clare gave her shoulders a nervous movement of disdain. "Oh yes, my music. I was going to be a pianist, you know."

"But you are!"

"Parlor music! I was going to be a great pianist."

Maggy fumbled again. "But marriage—a career . . ."

"It wasn't that. Look here." With a sweep, Clare shot up her full green sleeve and thrust out her arm. "See that." She turned and flexed the hard muscles.

There was, Maggy saw only then, the slightest kind of curve which was a little wrong, a little out of kilter. "I never noticed that!"

"No, you wouldn't. Nobody would. But it finished me as a pianist. Oh, don't look so sorry. It's long in the past." She lowered her sleeve and said in a faraway voice, "It was an accident."

The word was beginning to take on a certain disagreeable connotation, something almost more than accident. There had been an accident on the river. An accident, but two people had died. Clare was aware of that overtone, that slight significance, too, and gave Maggy a quick glance. "I mean, just an accident. Happened a long time ago. Kirk and I never got along—too much alike—furious tempers, both of us." She shot a glance at Maggy. "You know that, of course."

"No! That is, of course Kirk has a temper." Maggy thought for a moment. Clare examined a figure on the rug as if she had never seen it before. Maggy said, "But he controls it. He's kind and reasonable. He never lets his temper get the best of him."

"Well," Clare said, "one time in the middle of one of

our rows—it wasn't a scuffle—that's what Cousin Emily called it—it was a knock-down, drag-out fight, both of us in a white rage, beside ourselves—I fell on the stairs. Cousin Emily shot me straight to the best orthopedist she could find, but the bone never mended perfectly. So that was that."

It explained the little shadow of something which was not a frown, not even a tiny wrinkle, between Kirk's eyebrows, which was barely a look of discomfort in Kirk's face when, as Maggy sat with him on the terrace, Clare's music had rippled out from the house and then stopped with an abrupt crash.

Maggy said slowly, "That's dreadful, Clare. Kirk must blame himself. He'd never stop blaming himself."

"I suppose he does. And I never let him forget it, either. Oh, I'm mean, Maggy. Revengeful. I hold a grudge. At the same time"—she lifted that pale gaze to Maggy—"I'd do anything Kirk wants me to do, anything. It's that charm of his. He's my brother. If he wants to, he can twist me around his little finger, no matter how determined I am not to let him. You can't help it with Kirk," Clare said. "Well, I'd advise you to get some sleep. Oh, yes! There may be some discussion about the wedding— shall we change anything, make it a very quiet one, no reception, send wires to everybody—that kind of thing. Cousin Emily may fret a little. Ralph, and now Lydia. But Alroy says if we do change anything it'll cause more talk than if we go straight ahead with everything as planned. What's your feeling about it?"

"Why, we can't change anything now," Maggy said blankly.

"All right, then. We'll go straight on with everything just as planned. Best thing to do, of course. I'll cope with

Cousin Emily and everything. Good night, Maggy."

She went away quickly. Maggy glanced at the clock as she put out the light. It didn't seem possible that it was only a little after two-thirty, yet so much had happened since she had crept quietly out of the room to see Lydia.

It was hard to capture sleep. Small pictures, tiny segments of bigger pictures, presented themselves flashingly in her restless mind, and as flashingly gave place to others. The faint pink smear of lipstick on a wrinkled white pillowcase; had the shadow on Lydia's face pressed down into the other pillow been in fact a lingering, heavy, purplish flush? Maggy turned on her own pillow, which seemed hot and uncomfortable, and immediately saw the canoe gliding out from the fringe of willows with Lydia sitting so erect and firm, facing the house, with a nimbus of light from the sun around her hair.

Maggy tried the pillow still another way. All the same, in spite of everything Clare had said to explain Alroy, Maggy didn't really like Alroy and his slaty, sullen eyes.

Kirk had been angry, justifiably angry, when he talked to Josh and to Dr. Mason, but he hadn't been in what Clare had called a white rage, nothing like that at all.

Ralph Hewitt suddenly seemed to come diffidently up the steps to the terrace again, in his sagging seersucker suit. Where was Ralph? No, no, she wouldn't think of that. She'd think of—yes, tomorrow on the plane, winging through the night.

Something thumped hard against the screen across the room.

She sat up, startled. It was a moth, of course. It had thumped so hard that it had fallen to the terrace below, ending its small life.

She settled back again, but it wasn't a moth, for it

thumped again softly, yet hard and purposefully, too, like a messenger. Someone was standing down there on the terrace flinging something at the screen. She knew instantly that it was Josh.

She felt her way across the room, pressed her face against the screen and Josh whispered from below, "Maggy —Maggy . . ."

She could barely see the light oval of his face.

"Come down here," he whispered.

"No! No, I won't!"

"If you don't," Josh whispered promptly, "I'll come up there and get you."

He would come and get her, too. And Kirk would hear him and this time—this time, she thought with utter conviction—Kirk would make no allowances. The fat would be in the fire and no mistake about that.

"There's something I want you to see," Josh whispered. "Hurry up."

"Oh, all right," she snapped, forgetting to whisper but keeping her voice low, just the same. She groped in the darkness for her white robe; she felt her way out and into the hall. It was perfectly still; all the doors were closed. Alroy, she thought vaguely, must have returned, although she hadn't heard the car. She went down the stairs, as she had gone once before that night, again at Josh's imperative summons, to meet him at the front door. That seemed a long time ago, yet it was part of the same night and part of the same pattern.

Pattern, she thought sharply. Now what did she mean by that?

Nothing—nothing at all. She went through the living room and opened the French door. She held the screen carefully so it wouldn't creak. It was so dark on the terrace that she could barely see Josh sitting on the balustrade, but he saw her and came to her. "Thorniest damn roses I ever threw at a window. I really bled for your sake, Maggy. I thought you'd never wake up."

For a second, her dream of threatening roses growing too lush, rampant and strong, flashed back to her. So it was roses Josh had flung at the screen. "I wasn't asleep!"

He took her hand and led her toward the steps that went down to the lawn.

"Josh—no . . ."

"Go ahead and scream if you want to," he said, and drew her down onto the lawn, toward the path to the arbor.

The grass felt cold and wet under her thin bedroom slippers. She went beside him, fuming. He knew that she wouldn't scream and wake the house—wake Kirk.

Josh said, "Look out, here's the path."

A night fog had come down following the rain; the leaves reached out cold fingers along either side of the path and brushed wetly over her face. The slight rustle of shrubbery as Josh led her upward along the narrow path sounded loud. It was very still and very dark, yet the woods and the clumps of laurels and roses, invisible in the darkness, made their presence felt. It was as if something listened to their footsteps.

Gradually a dull murmur began to emerge from the darkness and the silence; it was the river, of course, so they were getting near the lookout point. Josh said, "Here we are."

It was still dark; Maggy thought the fog must be very thick, but she had a sense of being in the open again. Josh said, "Don't move. We're near the edge of the rocks. . . ." There was a click and the flame of his cigarette lighter shot up.

122

It made a small but dazzling tongue of light. Beyond it, all around them, the darkness became blacker, although there was a faint silver reflection shimmering in the dense fog. Josh held the lighter as if it were a candle. She could see his brown hand clearly, and the lines of it, and the light blur of his shirt. He led the way to the arbor, and she followed him. "Look," he said, and held the lighter higher.

It lit up the interior of the arbor waveringly, but clearly enough. The two rustic chairs had been pushed together. A crumpled blue and white blanket lay across one of them. A bottle of whiskey stood beside the chairs.

Josh said, "George must have been here sleeping off his tippling or"—he touched the whiskey bottle with the toe of one moccasin—"going in for tippling on a larger scale. The point is, why did he leave—and when? Before Lydia died or afterward?"

"I knew you weren't going to stop! Now you're going to say George murdered Lydia!"

Josh's chin caught a point of light; above it his eyes were in the shadow. "Well," he said reasonably, "somebody killed her. Maybe it was George."

ELEVEN

"No! Josh, can't you admit you're wrong?"

"No, I can't," Josh said coolly. "There's not much time. I've got to talk to George. I'd like to know whether or not he was in the house tonight."

"If he was I didn't see him. But"—she hesitated and said unwillingly—"Someone could have come into the house. The French door in the living room was open. I mean, when you left me there and went up to see Lydia. And there was a candle burning on the terrace—but that was earlier."

"When?"

"I saw it when I woke up. There was just a sort of glow down on the terrace. I looked, and one of the hurricane candles—we'd left them on the balustrade after dinner—one of them was still lighted. I thought it was queer because it had rained. But I went to Lydia's room and—then I called the doctor and you came. You went upstairs. It was then that I found the terrace door open, but the candle had gone out. The terrace was dark."

Josh considered it. "I suppose George could have brought the blanket down from the house early in the evening. Then—oh, perhaps he woke up, decided he wanted another drink and went down to the house, found the candle, lighted it, found the door still open, went in, helped himself to whiskey—yes, he could have done all that." The small light wavered as he looked down at her. "But did he go to Lydia's room?"

"I don't know! I'm going back to the house. . . ."

"You're going to stay right here. I've got something I want to say to you." He snapped off the lighter. In the darkness he pulled her down into one of the rustic chairs, fumbled with the blanket and put it around her. He discovered her feet, chilled and wet, and held them in his hands for a moment. "Smart girl," he said derisively. "Coming out on this thorny path in such thin slippers."

"I'm not going to listen to anything you want to say. There isn't any question of murder. . . ."

"There are so many questions, my little friend, that they would make your head spin." He wrapped the blanket around her feet and sat in the other chair, so close to her that she could feel the pressure of his arm. "I was sent here to investigate Kirk and the Beall Company."

"What are you talking about?"

"It's simple. Kirk is getting out a new and a big stock issue. He may have told you something about it. The usual routine is, of course, through an underwriter and the brokerage houses. The bigger and better the firm which accepts the stock for sale, the better for Kirk. Eventually, of course, he expects to get his stock okayed by the SEC and on an exchange."

"I know that! Everybody knows it!"

"Yes—well, there are certain qualifications. The point is, there is some question as to whether or not the Beall Company is up to its claims. That is, whether or not there is fraud or attempted fraud."

"Kirk!" she laughed. "That's absurd. Why—besides everything else he's too intelligent."

"You'd be surprised how many smart people have tried

125

it and proved themselves not so smart. I came back last week, went to get my old brokerage job back. My boss knows that I live in Milrock. So I was asked to come up and see what I could find out before any report is submitted to the SEC."

"You mean, to spy on Kirk!"

"That's what it amounts to," Josh said coolly. "Of course, everything may be perfectly honest and on the level. Nobody could put a finger on any specific flaws. But there are ways of finagling. The Beall Company is growing but there's a—a doubt as to whether or not it is growing as fast as they claim. Their financial statements seem a little too impressive—just possibly faked."

"How could anybody fake a financial statement?"

"Oh, a number of ways," Josh said rather dryly. "That's what I was sent here to find out—if I can. Nobody wants to make an issue, or an official thing of it at this time. The idea is that I may be able to get a line on something."

"Spying," she said again.

"If the Beall outfit is trying to pull a fast one, it's better for everybody to stop it now, isn't it? Better for Kirk. Certainly better for Miss Emily and all of them. I did take some time to think before I said I would," Josh said soberly. "What it summed up to was this: if everything is all right, that's good. If it isn't, I just might be able to make it easier for them. That is, I can't tip Kirk off, of course. But if I didn't take on the job, somebody else would. It would be somebody who didn't know the Bealls or didn't care. It might even be somebody who would have to go at it openly so everybody would know about it, everybody in Milbridge, everybody on Wall Street."

"That's why you wanted to visit the works. Are you going to ask to see their accounts? Are you going to ask to check on their bank deposits?" she said with sharp sarcasm.

Josh replied literally. "I can't do anything like that. It's not my job. Besides, they've had accountants, and a good firm. Kirk would see to that. But accountants have had the wool pulled over their eyes before now. There's the old saying, figures don't lie but liars can figure."

"What are you going to do then?"

"What I was told to do. Look around, feel my way, talk to people . . ."

"Snoop!"

"All right, snoop. Visit the plant, ask questions, talk to stockholders, talk to workmen, talk to townspeople. Keep my eyes and ears open. Oh, it's an intangible kind of thing, like trying to find a trail you're not sure is there. I'm sure I hope it isn't there," Josh said with a sigh. "But once they found out I knew the Bealls, it was put to me squarely. It's my job, but it's also—well, I had to. I don't expect you to understand."

There was a long silence. Finally Maggy said coldly, "Well, what have you done?"

"Not much. I spent yesterday, before I came here, in Milbridge. I wasn't cut out for this sort of work. The freight agent knew about how much the works shipped and didn't mind talking about it, proud of it. But that wasn't very conclusive or suggestive. I went to school with Harry Simmons, who works at the bank. We had lunch together. Not a peep out of him, of course, except that the plant is booming. I talked to several other people. I've been away, you see, so it wasn't hard to get the conversation around to changes, new business and all that. Everybody gave the Beall Company a big hand. They have got out various new lines. One of them is a packaged do-it-yourself kind of kit, small tools in one package for amateur carpenters or just anybody who owns a house and likes to do repairs, that sort of thing. It's going like hotcakes."

"You admit the Beall Company is booming."

"Maggy, I'm not the president of the Stock Exchange! I'm not a partner of Baller and Yule. I'm just trying to do a job—and I've got special reasons for trying to do it. I hope that Kirk and the works and the whole thing are on the level. And if there should be something wrong in the setup, maybe I'm not smart enough to see it. I have no official status whatever. I don't even know exactly how to go about it. All I can do is—well, try. This is all unofficial and before any report goes to the SEC."

"You'll not find anything wrong."

"I don't expect to find anything specific—anything that's in black and white. It's only straws I'm looking for."

"Straws!" she said derisively.

Josh ignored it. "If there is any funny business going on, Kirk's not the only one in on it. George Clowe seems to be his right hand, in his confidence. Alroy might be in on it—or he might have sufficient cause for suspicion to be a danger to Kirk. Kirk is buying him and Clare a new house in Milbridge."

"Do you mean you think that's—that's like blackmail? It isn't. It's just Kirk. He's kind and generous. He's buying Miss Emily a house, too, if she wants one. . . ."

"I know," Josh said. "In Switzerland."

"This is why you are so opposed to my marriage," she said slowly.

"Part of the reason. I don't want your husband hauled off to jail."

"That's not going to happen."

"The rest of the reason is—I still believe that Lydia was

murdered. And I think that Kirk may be a killer and he may be a crook."

"That is not true, Josh."

"Are you going to marry him on Thursday? Or will you wait . . . ?"

"Josh, you must be reasonable. When you said it was murder tonight, Kirk instantly had it all out in the open. He asked your father. . . ."

"What else could he have done? No, wait. I'll tell you what he could have done. He could have called the police and asked for an investigation."

"Police," she cried. "Headlines. Everything—just before our wedding! And there's no evidence of murder, nothing to investigate!" She started to her feet but Josh's hand shot out and gripped her wrist.

"Stay here. You're an ostrich, Maggy. Sticking your head in the sand. Determined on this fine wedding . . ."

"I believe in Kirk. And I'm in love with him."

"Are you?" Josh said and turned her toward him. He drew her nearer, she could feel the warmth of his cheek upon her own. Something like a swift kind of spark seemed to light between them and she had to put it out, now and forever. She pulled herself away and up from the chair. She thrust away the blanket that entangled itself around her feet. "No," she said, "that's not fair."

Josh had not moved. He said soberly from the close darkness, "Perhaps it isn't fair. But that's the way it is between us."

"No." She had moved to the open side of the arbor without knowing it. The sound of the river was clear. Her hand brushed against one of the old corner posts. She said, "I'm as good as married to Kirk."

"Not yet."

"But I am. I made up my mind to it. I was sure—I am sure. I've promised. I am as fully committed as if we were already married. I'm not going to change on an impulse. Because of a—an attraction that doesn't mean anything."

"It does to me. I got my eyes open tonight."

"You don't mean that. You let Kirk think that but . . ."

"It's the truth," Josh said slowly. "I had to weigh my future against yours. I had to decide whether you or my job is most important to me. So I made a little bet with myself. I flipped a quarter and it came up for my job. But it didn't work out that way. I had to choose your future. That's how I knew."

"Your future . . ."

"Oh, Maggy, get your head out of the sand. If Kirk finds out, or if you tell him why I'm here, I'm useless. I'll have to go back to the office and say, sorry, but I got involved in personal feelings, Kirk Beall found out what I was trying to do. I had to give up the whole thing. In short if I want to keep my job—and I like it and I do want to keep it—then I've got to shut up and let you go ahead and marry a man who may be a crook and may be a killer. I can't. I discovered it then. I'm in love with you. I don't know when it happened or how but now I know what I'm going to do."

She heard the chair move as he rose and came to her. She moved back against the arbor. "No," she said. "No! My marriage is settled. It's important. I'm the same as married now, really. I've made up my mind, Josh. So I'm not going to see you again. I'm not going to listen to you. I beg you to give up this dreadful idea of yours. . . ."

"Hasn't it occurred to you that you are in danger?"

"Danger . . ."

"You found Lydia and you can't say definitely that there was no cyanosis. You heard Lydia say, 'He tried to kill me.' You're a witness. . . ."

"You heard that, too!"

"My testimony, that of one person, could be put aside. Your testimony backing me up, corroborative evidence, couldn't be put aside. I didn't want you to tell anybody that you heard her say that, Maggy."

"But—why . . . ?"

"I tried to will you not to tell but you would do it. You've got to understand. There is no murder case without you. If I were the murderer," Josh said soberly, "I'd be scared. And I'd know that I'd never be safe until I'd got rid of you. Never. Weeks, months—years from now. Except it would be dangerous to wait too long."

"I—don't believe . . ." Something, though, did believe and touched her like a chill little wind, coming out of the darkness. There was a kind of rustle, somewhere near the arbor, as if a wind, like fear, had touched the roses, too.

"You don't want to believe," Josh said. "I'm going to see if that's George prowling around behind the arbor."

TWELVE

She heard it, too, again, a slight rustle, as if some creature of the woods were moving stealthily in the woods behind the arbor. Except it was not a small night creature, for a twig snapped distantly. No hunting owl, no soft-footed rabbit or mole, not even a marauding woodchuck, would tread so incautiously.

Josh vanished into the fog. She heard him call, "George —George . . ." Apparently he went up through the woods. Gradually the little crackle of twigs and rustle of undergrowth diminished.

She wouldn't wait for Josh. She would have to see him again, but not alone. She wouldn't listen to him again. Even in listening there was a disloyalty to Kirk.

The fog was so heavy that it blotted out the rim of the lookout point and the entrance of the path to the house. The corner post and the scent of the roses were like a compass point in a bewildering sea. She clung to the arbor for a second and then left it and ventured out away from it, taking a line toward the entrance to the path. It was so dark that she could not even distinguish a darker line of shrubbery.

She found that, however. A branch laden with wet leaves swept her face. But in the bewildering fog and darkness she missed the opening to the path. She groped for it, encountered only wet foliage and thrusting branches, decided that she had gone too far toward the east and moved in the darkness toward the west and still there was no opening in the wall of branches and leaves. It was as if the path itself had disappeared. She moved back, she moved forward and suddenly she was lost.

She stopped. It seemed to her then, abruptly, that the ripple of the river was very clear—too clear. She must be near the edge of the lookout point.

That was dangerous. Josh had talked of danger. Josh was wrong. But there was a danger in the blackness and the rim of the rocks, which must be altogether too near her and was completely masked in the fog and the darkness. A careless misstep, a move in the wrong direction, that was the danger. She could go down, down and down into the river and no one would ever know.

She waited, trying to orient herself in a place she had known all her life and yet was suddenly strange and frightening. She tried to see through the black fog veils. There was not even a dim outline of the arbor. The murmur of the river was confusing, too; it seemed to surge all around her, so she could not be sure of its direction.

If she could discover the line of shrubbery again, she had only to follow it back, away from the river, toward the hillside, to arrive at the opening of the path.

But where exactly was the shrubbery? Her hands groped out into a black void. And just then a shadow did seem to detach itself from the blackness and take on a kind of vague and wavering outline.

Josh? Nobody. She was mistaken. There was no one there, no sound, nothing but fog shapes. Certainly no one called to her, no one spoke. Something brushed her hand and she nearly screamed and it was only a bramble.

She caught the scream back in her throat, with a gasp of

133

relief. The line of shrubbery was exactly here. All she had to do was edge along it, carefully, never losing touch of one wet branch and then another so she wouldn't again lose her sense of direction, and she would find the path.

She did so cautiously, almost holding her breath, waiting to make sure before she took one step and then another. She could hear nothing above the ripple of the river, not even the slight rustle of her own slow progress from one clump of shrubbery to another. She thought that she must be almost at the opening of the path where the wet leaves and branches would give way, and paused. Something clattered lightly and sharply, somewhere in the blackness near her.

It was only a rock, a small rock, clattering down over the edge of the lookout point toward the river. She could hear it strike sharply against other rocks. The small, sharp sound diminished, stopped altogether.

But rocks don't dislodge themselves and go bouncing down, striking other rocks, dropping at last into the river! There *was* someone on the lookout point. All her senses clamored a discovery: Josh was right. Murder, evidence of murder—danger. In that moment she believed him.

She crouched back into the thick laurels and tried not to breathe. There was no sound at all except the murmur of the river.

After a long time she thought, clearly, rocks *do* fall of themselves. It had sounded like a small rock, scarcely more than a pebble. Probably she had dislodged it herself, as she turned away from the edge of the rocks.

After a longer time, gradually, she was certain that there was no one, no one at all, there on the lookout point or in the arbor. Panic, that was all. Panic and the fog and darkness.

She moved, cautiously and listening still, but moved and nothing came from the black sea around her, nobody moved, no hands came groping through the laurels. Suddenly the touch of wet foliage gave out, ended, and she had found the path.

As she turned into it, a car started up with a roar, down at the house. The sound was muffled by distance and fog but it was the sound of an engine starting and it was real, no fancied sound in the dark. Almost immediately, too, there were shouts, muffled and far away, but real, too.

She ran down the path, guiding herself by the trees and brambles on either side, bumping against low branches and foliage which shook drops like rain on her face, disentangling herself from brambles which came out of the darkness as if they would have stopped her. But no ghostly steps raced along the path behind her. No stealthy presence kept pace with her through the woods. In seconds, it seemed to her, so wild and precipitate had been her flight, she emerged onto the lawn.

The house stood, lighted here and there, like a ship on a late night sea. She ran across the wet lawn and up on the terrace. Only then she turned to look over her shoulder. No one came running after her, out of the fog.

Afraid of the dark, she told herself derisively. Afraid of something which had not even been a shadow. Afraid of a rock, a pebble, clattering down to the river. She crossed the terrace and opened the French door. Inside the living room she paused.

Light was streaking in from the hall. Men's voices, low, were coming from the dining room. She followed the lane of light across the room and into the hall where she stopped. She didn't want to see anyone; she didn't want anyone, especially Kirk, to see her. She would run lightly, so no one would know, up the stairs to the haven of her room and stay there until she was entirely herself again, not a child afraid of fancies born of the dark.

Alroy's voice came from the dining room. ". . . so we tried to find you. Where have you been?"

Kirk said, "Take it easy, George."

And then George said, in a muffled, uneven voice, "I can't understand it—I can't understand it. . . ."

So they told him.

The stairway itself protected her; she couldn't see into the dining room from there and no one could see her. She had only to edge up the stairs, keeping close to the wall.

Kirk, though, heard her. He came along the hall quickly and saw her halfway up the stairs, clinging to the railing. "Maggy! What are you . . . ?" His glance took in her wet and disheveled hair, her draggled, white silk dressing gown. He stared at her, his face incredulous, and then came up to meet her. "What have you been doing? What's happened? You're frightened. . . ."

She clung to him thankfully. This was the haven she wanted. This was the warmth and safety.

But she had to answer Kirk. She mumbled against his shoulder, "I went up to the lookout point."

His arms stiffened with surprise. "At this time of night?"

She had to say something. "Josh thought that he had found George. At least, he'd found—he thought George had been there—there was a blanket and . . ."

"Of course George was there." Kirk drew her down the few steps and held her a little away from him so the light fell full on her face. "George went up there this evening. That's why we couldn't find him. We never thought of looking there."

"He's here now. . . ."

"Yes, of course. He came down from the arbor and got into his car a few moments ago. We've told him about Lydia. Why did Josh take *you* to the arbor? Why didn't he come for me? For that matter, what business of Josh's . . ."

"George wasn't there, you see, so we waited. . . ." It was not an answer to anything.

The little line between Kirk's eyebrows showed that it was no answer. He waited a moment, then drew her back into the living room. "I don't understand this. Do you mean to say that simply because Josh told you to, you left the house, you went up to the arbor . . . ?"

"George. He wanted to find George."

Kirk brushed it away. "He wanted to talk to you. Maggy, we've got to have an understanding about this. I love you. I've never wanted a woman before in my life. Perhaps I'm possessive, too possessive. But I want you. I'll never let you go. Josh, perhaps because you've known him so long, seems to have a very strong influence over you. I don't say that it's a bad influence. But I don't think it's—well, a sensible influence. I'm going to stop it."

She was in the wrong; she was entirely in the wrong, yet contrarily she had an impulse to defend Josh, as when Josh attacked Kirk she must defend Kirk. "Josh is an old friend, he wouldn't, he hasn't . . ."

"I'll deal with Josh. You are my wife—the same as my wife even now—and I'm going to take care of you. And I'll also, Maggy, keep my own . . ." He stopped as the terrace door rattled.

Josh opened it, came in, seemed to pause and observe them standing together in the path of light from the hall. He said, after a second or two, "Oh. I just wanted to make sure you got back to the house, Maggy."

He guessed that she had told Kirk that she had been at the lookout point with him. Josh was in the shadow, but it seemed to Maggy that his eyes surveyed her and Kirk very thoughtfully.

He said, "I didn't mean to leave you there so long, Maggy. George—or somebody—was right ahead of me, going through the woods. He wouldn't stop but I could hear him. I chased after him, down the hill again to the highway. Couldn't see anybody there so I went back to the arbor. I'm sorry." He turned back to the door; he was going to leave.

Kirk said abruptly and harshly, "Wait, Josh. I've something to say to you."

Josh's eyebrows went up a little. He shoved his hands into his pockets, but waited. Kirk turned to Maggy, and kissed her, and gave her a little push toward the stairs. Josh, in the shadows, observed it all.

Kirk watched at the foot of the stairs; at the top she turned, and he was still watching, the light full on his face. It was as if he said again, "You're my wife—the same as my wife—and I'm going to take care of you. And I'll keep what is mine. . . ."

Kirk was the haven and Kirk was the refuge. Something cold and frightened, a memory of fog and darkness, a memory of a moment when she had believed Josh—actually in her heart believed him—and believed murder and danger, disappeared, vanished, floated away as if it had never been. She went into her room.

But she did not turn on the light. She went across the room to the bay window above the terrace. She must hear, if she could, what Kirk said to Josh and what Josh said to Kirk, and it was so direct and somehow so important a need that not the faintest scruple about eavesdropping

138

touched her. She pressed her face against the screen and waited, and after only a moment or two—so they couldn't have quarreled—they came out on the terrace below. The door rattled and closed, and she could hear their footsteps. Kirk's voice floated up, disembodied in the fog and darkness. ". . . so you do understand."

Josh said something; it sounded like an assent. They seemed to walk toward the far end of the terrace and the steps leading to the path which went around the house toward the front. Kirk said quite clearly, "I do realize that Maggy is very fond of you, naturally. I don't interfere with your friendship. But taking her up to the arbor in the middle of the night and leaving her there . . ."

"It's almost morning," Josh said clearly and factually. "And anyway, she got back all right."

But I was terrified just the same, Maggy thought. Afraid of a shadow, but afraid.

Kirk said gravely, "You do see my point of view?"

"Indeed I do," Josh said. There was only the slightest edge in his voice, so slight that apparently Kirk did not detect it, for he said, "I thought you would. Good night, Josh."

Josh said something. Kirk's footsteps came back along the terrace. The door opened and closed again.

For a second or two, something chill and desolate came from the fog and the blackness. Kirk didn't know it and she would never tell him—Josh knew but did not believe her—but she knew that in that instant Josh had walked down from the terrace and out of her life.

It was the way it should be, it was the way she had chosen. It was her own decision—yet in fact there had been no decision to make for her course, her marriage was already decided upon. She was a woman, not a child to be

139

swayed by a moment's fancy. That was the way she wanted it to be.

She would see Josh, of course; she might even be aware of him, in the church among others, watching her as she took the vows, which actually she felt as if she had taken weeks ago when she promised to marry Kirk. Josh might even come to the house after the wedding, she might touch his hand when he came along the little receiving line. But that was all.

Another decision reinforced itself. She would never tell Kirk any of the things Josh had said to her. She would never tell him that Josh had said that Kirk might be a crook and a killer. She would never tell him that Josh had said he loved her.

She wouldn't tell him, either, she thought presently, that Josh had come to Milrock to investigate the Beall Company. She hadn't promised Josh not to tell it, but she felt obscurely that she owed Josh that confidence. And it was not disloyal to Kirk, for Josh would find nothing wrong.

She was cold. She dropped her dressing gown over a chair and felt her way to the bed where she huddled thankfully under the blankets.

For a moment, only a moment, she had believed Josh and believed that murder was abroad in the night. The plain fact was that clumsily she had got herself turned around in directions and nearly had an accident. Accident! There was the word again.

But it was accident—or nearly. The rest of it existed only in her fancy. Nobody had stood in the darkness close to her. Nobody had approached her. Nobody had given her even the slightest thrust downward into the murmurous and deadly blackness of the river far below.

The river still seemed to ripple and murmur in her ears;

140

it became bewildering, near and then far away again, gradually farther and farther.

Emily awakened her. "Maggy! I don't like to call you, but it's nearly eleven-thirty and the rehearsal is at twelve. Maggy, wake up, dear."

THIRTEEN

Maggy opened her eyes. Emily was standing beside the bed, neat to the last gray curl, crisp in a pink linen dress. She had a cup of coffee in her hand. "I really didn't like to call you, but rehearsal—drink this, Maggy."

A breakfast tray stood on the table. Maggy thrust herself up against the pillows and took the cup of coffee. Emily said, "The Graham baby has a cold and can't be christened this morning as was planned, so the church is free for rehearsal, and of course I said that we'd be delighted to have the rehearsal at noon. Much better than later. I phoned Kirk—he went to the office early this morning—and he and Alroy will meet us at the church. He couldn't get hold of the ushers but that doesn't matter. Are you sure you're awake, dear?"

Maggy nodded over her first revivifying gulp of coffee. The room was full of a soft, dull gray light. Emily's crisp neatness, her matter-of-fact manner, drove away any dark fancies of the night. Emily said, "I'll run the tub for you," and went briskly into the bathroom.

She came back. "You won't go back to sleep again now," she said.

"No. Really, I'm awake. Thanks . . ."

"I'll go on ahead to the church then and talk to the organist. I'll take Mrs. Elwell. She can't get away for the wedding so she wants to see the rehearsal. Clare will bring you." She went out. There was no difference in her at all that morning unless she was a little firmer, a little more decisive.

However, it set the pattern. They were going to go on as if nothing had happened, as if the police were not searching the river for the body of Ralph Hewitt, and as if there had been no tragic, unexpected death in the night.

She wondered how Clare had effected it. Perhaps Clare had needed to do nothing; perhaps everyone instantly saw and agreed that that was the only possible course.

In any event, the night was past, and now in the light of day, after what had in fact been a deep, long sleep, and in the middle of a second cup of coffee, Maggy remembered with complete astonishment that there had been a moment, even a second, during the night when she had believed murder. Just for a moment, a second, she had believed that she herself was in danger!

She ate hurriedly and dashed to dress. She paused once to glance from the window. The fog still hung on, pearly gray and opaque, shrouding the trees and hovering so close about the river that she could not even distinguish a line between the fog and the river. She fastened the belt of her blue cotton dress. She paused again for a moment and adjusted a shimmering silk fold of her wedding dress. She fluffed out the veil. It's beautiful, she thought unexpectedly, as if she had never seen it before, as if it had nothing to do with her.

Then she hurried for the stairs and absurdly, all at once, she seemed to be two people.

One was Maggy, going down the stairs to meet Clare and clamber into Clare's little car. Clare said, "Filthy day." Maggy said, "Yes." This was Maggy the bride, going to her wedding rehearsal.

143

Another Maggy, though, seemed to accompany her, eyeing the first Maggy as she had eyed the wedding dress, remotely as if she were an observer. She seemed to listen, too, sharply, when Maggy said, "Have they found Ralph?"

"No," Clare said, and after a pause, "I'm glad we're getting this foggy weather over with. It will clear up and be sunny tomorrow."

Tomorrow, Maggy thought, my wedding day.

Fog moistened the windshield and the windows; Clare turned on the windshield wiper, which thrust back and forth regularly. A truck swished past them. The pavement was black and wet and the green foliage along the roadside glistened. When they turned into the main street of Milrock, lights were on in the stores; the fog pressed down over the great oaks that lined the streets. In spite of the foggy day, Main Street seemed unusually active; there were little knots of people outside the broad, lighted windows of the stores and on the steps of the old red brick post office, talking. It seemed to Maggy that the clusters of people fell silent as they passed, and turned to watch them.

But the whole of Milrock knew of the canoe accident and, by now, of Lydia's death. All of Milrock knew of the wedding, and most of Milrock would be in the church the next day.

The church stood in the middle of a little green. Its white steeple went up into the fog, and shining green ivy draped its gray stone walls. It was dimly lighted, too. Kirk's car was already parked in the street before it.

Clare and Maggy went up the neat brick walk, edged with myrtle, along which Maggy had trotted many times as a child. Inside the church, Emily, Kirk and Alroy stood down at the altar railing talking to the minister, Dr. Norris; he had a tanned face, a crew cut and a serious expression as he nodded, apparently in agreement with Emily's directions. Kirk saw them and came to meet them. His black head was lifted, his eyes lighted and smiling. He took her hand and kissed her lightly. "Darling," he whispered. She knew that the others were watching and thinking, the bride and groom, an ideal couple, a perfect wedding.

The organ boomed suddenly through the little church, and after a kind of practice run of pipes and pedals, shot into the wedding march. Mrs. Elwell, in a large black hat, rose from a pew and made repressive gestures at the organist, who checked the organ with a crashing thump.

"Now then," Emily said, and called them. "Kirk, you and Alroy in the vestry. Clare and Maggy back in the vestibule." She waited until Kirk and Alroy had disappeared into the vestry, with the door just slightly ajar and Alroy peering out, and until Clare and Maggy had retreated to the vestibule. Young Dr. Norris had disappeared, too, but was watching discreetly from the door at the opposite side of the altar. Emily waved one white-gloved hand at the organist, who did not appear to see it, and Mrs. Elwell obligingly, and in a startling deep alto, sang, "Here—comes—the bride . . ."

The organist took up her admonitory signal and the refrain. Clare gave a nervous laugh. "Follow me when Cousin Emily signals. About ten steps behind me. We'll both have on high heels. I only hope I don't fall on my face trying to keep step with the organ. I wish she'd make it faster—there—there's Kirk and Alroy and Dr. Norris all at the altar. Here I go. . . ." It didn't seem real.

It was real though. There was the pew where she had sat long ago beside her mother and tried to be quiet and counted the bald heads in the congregation and then the

145

people wearing spectacles and by then had gone to sleep. She could remember the flowery light scent of her mother's perfume. The church was lighted only by a few sconce lights along the walls, between the arched windows which that day were gray with fog. She was counting Clare's steps—eight, nine, ten, now!

As she started down the aisle, there was a long swish and sigh, so she knew that the big, main door of the church had opened and closed. She was vaguely aware that someone tiptoed across the vestibule behind her and apparently settled down in a pew at the back. The familiar measured notes of the wedding march echoed hollowly through the church. Tomorrow the church would be full of people; tomorrow there would be a little buzz and hum and rustle as people turned to watch the bride. There would be light summer dresses and hats, the formal dark coats of the men. She was getting too far from Clare, she was walking too slowly; she hastened her steps a little and then checked herself as she got out of time with the music. Clare was right; it was difficult to walk so slowly. She was getting an odd kind of stage fright. Tomorrow it would be easier, wouldn't it—in her shimmering white dress with its cloudy white veil? Or would it be harder?

Emily whispered piercingly, "There! Stop just there, beside Kirk."

She stopped. She felt the pressure of Kirk's arm against her own. The young minister faced them. Clare had stepped a little to one side. Somebody, Emily perhaps, or Mrs. Elwell, who certainly seemed to supply a kind of expertise about church weddings (how many weddings had she witnessed in that little church?) appeared to be making imperative motions toward the organist who, however, was watching the whole thing in her mirror now, Maggy knew, and came to a solemn chord and stopped. There was a little hush. Dr. Norris said cheerfully, "And then the ceremony—'Dearly beloved, we are gathered together'—and so on and so on, until we come to 'Who giveth this woman to be married to this man?'" He paused uncertainly and looked at Emily. "I don't believe—who is to give the bride away?"

It was a hitch. It was a sudden and shocking hitch. Nobody spoke for a second; everybody seemed frozen. Then there was a rustle as Emily rose. "Why, that—that was to be George Clowe."

Kirk turned to look at Emily. Alroy seemed obscurely amused; his slaty eyes were bright. Clare said nervously, "I forgot about that, I simply forgot—I'm sorry. . . ."

Kirk said to Emily, "It's all right." He glanced around the church and his face cleared. He turned to the minister. "I expect you've heard about . . ."

"Oh, yes," young Dr. Norris said quickly, and passed one hand over his crew cut. "I'm so sorry. You have everybody's sympathy. Especially—well, in the circumstances . . ."

Emily had got her firmness back again. She said, "We'll just skip that part of it, can't we?"

Maggy's memory shot back to all the discussion about it. Should Alroy give her away? No, that wouldn't do; he was a member of Kirk's family. Well, then, who? Someone, Clare and Emily between them, had suggested George Clowe, and it was settled. Maggy herself, lost in her private rosy dreams, had listened absently; it seemed an unimportant detail.

Kirk said now, promptly, "It's not necessary to omit it at all. I'm sure Dr. Mason will be delighted—as a matter of fact, I don't know why we didn't think of him in the

147

first place. He's known Maggy most of her life. And he's certainly given away brides before now, so there's no need for him to rehearse. Is that all right with you, Maggy?"

She nodded but she was a little confused and obscurely troubled. Kirk turned to the back of the church and called clearly, "Josh, will you stand in for your father just for rehearsal?"

Josh, Maggy thought. So it was Josh who had entered the church as she was going down the aisle. No, no, she thought wildly, I will not march along that aisle with Josh, I will not talk to Josh, I will not so much as look at him! I decided all that last night.

But Josh, unusually elegant again in dark gray slacks and a blue sports coat, was strolling down the aisle. "Yes, of course, I'll be delighted," he said coolly.

Everything settled itself neatly, calmly. Emily sank back into the pew and gave directions to start all over again. Maggy and Clare and Josh trudged back to the vestibule, Alroy and Kirk back to the vestry, Dr. Norris back to his own discreet lurking place. The organ began again. Clare flung back her mass of black hair and started the slow march down to the altar. Josh whispered, "You've got to take my arm, you know."

"No. I don't want to. I won't."

"Why not?"

She would not mince words. "Because you said Kirk was a crook and a killer. Because you said—I told you last night. I'm not going to listen."

"You can't help listening. I said he might be a crook and a killer. And I said I love you."

Clare wobbled, trying to restrain her swift nervous energy to the measured tum-tum-ti-tum of the organ. She

148

grasped the back of a pew to steady herself. Maggy thought, I can do that tomorrow. If tomorrow in that billowing white silk and in high heels she found herself unsteady, she could simply put her white-gloved hand on the back of a pew, clutch her bridal bouquet firmly with the other hand, and then go on. It wouldn't look very graceful. Did brides always think of such absurd contingencies?

Josh said, suddenly, with a throb of anger in his voice, "Every time I think that you're beginning to let me pound a little sense into that stubborn head of yours, Kirk charms you back again."

"That's not true! And I'm not going to let you even— even pretend to give me away. I'm not going to walk down that aisle with you!"

Josh exasperatingly chuckled. "Clare's halfway to the altar. Shouldn't we be starting? Now take my arm. . . ."

He extended his arm with only slightly exaggerated formality. Emily was already looking over her shoulder, fidgeting. Clare was almost at the altar. She had to put her hand on Josh's arm.

She could feel its warmth and strength through his blue linen sleeve. She tried to make her fingers light, barely touching the sleeve and Josh knew it. He put his other hand close and hard upon her own. She couldn't pull her hand away, even if she wanted to. But she did want to! Certainly she wanted to!

Josh said, "All right, now, let's get our steps together. One—two . . ." They started together down the aisle. Josh said in a low yet terrifyingly clear voice, so the organ music itself seemed to recede, "Relax. You've not going to marry Kirk. You're going to marry me."

FOURTEEN

This time everything went well; everyone did the proper thing; everyone stood in the prescribed spot—or so Maggy supposed. Josh retired at the correct moment to a pew opposite Emily's. Dr. Norris told the bride and groom where to kneel. Clare told Alroy to be sure not to drop the ring. Emily wiped her eyes and Mrs. Elwell sniffed emotionally.

"And after I pronounce you man and wife," Dr. Norris said, smiling at Kirk, "you kiss your bride."

Kirk laughed a little, exultantly, put his arm around Maggy, tilted her chin up and kissed her.

Josh sneezed raucously, reverberatingly, and said, "I am so sorry," loudly, too.

Kirk lifted his head. The minister gave Josh a rather reproving glance and said, "And that's it! Then you walk up the aisle. . . ."

The organist boomed into triumphant, singing chords. Kirk drew Maggy's arm close through his own, turned her around and they marched briskly past Emily, past Josh, up the aisle again.

"This," Kirk said, "is the real wedding. The first time a man and woman walk back up the aisle together. You're my wife, darling. Don't you feel that, too?"

I don't feel anything, Maggy thought, except I wish

Josh weren't here. I wish I hadn't had to walk with him, close to him, down the aisle. She said, "I don't know."

"I know." They had reached the end of the aisle and Kirk faced her, his eyes compelling in their bright exultance. "I've got the license in my pocket. I've got the ring. I got it out of the safe at the office this morning. Let's go straight back and be married right now. In three minutes—come on, Maggy."

"Oh, but—you're joking."

"I'm not joking at all. I'll go now and tell them that we're going to do it all over again but this time the whole ceremony, all of it. . . ."

"Oh, Kirk, you can't. There's—there's the reception and all the wedding guests and . . ."

"None of that matters. Clare can send them telegrams and tell them not to come. Look." They had gone on out of the church proper and into the small vestibule. The doors behind them were open. Maggy glanced back along the length of aisle and empty pews with their high white backs. Down at the altar Emily and Mrs. Elwell, Clare and Dr. Norris were in a huddle, talking. Alroy slumped on the railing and stared at nothing. Josh still sat in the pew looking straight ahead—so stiffly straight ahead that Maggy was sure he was listening, straining his ears toward the vestibule where she and Kirk stood. Kirk pulled a white box from his pocket and opened it.

"Oh!" Maggy said. A wide but lacy band of platinum, set with a pattern of small emeralds, was wedged into the jeweler's box.

"The stones match your engagement ring." Kirk took her left hand and looked at it. Suddenly the tiny line came between his eyebrows. "You're not wearing it."

"No, I've—I've been unpacking wedding gifts. All that

excelsior. I was afraid I'd lose it." The fact was that the emerald in her engagement ring was so big and, she was sure, so expensive that she couldn't bring herself to wear it all the time; indeed, most of the time it remained in its own white velvet box in a drawer.

Kirk slid the wedding ring on her finger. "Do you like it?"

"It's beautiful!" The emeralds winked with deep flashes of green fire.

"We'll go straight back to the altar. In a few minutes it will be on your finger forever."

"Oh, Kirk, you don't really want to!"

"You mean *you* don't want to," Kirk said suddenly, in a voice which she didn't know and yet knew and recognized, for she knew without looking at him that the tiny line was back between his eyebrows.

She fumbled at the wedding ring, trying to pull it from her fingers. "But we can't have the real ceremony now—there're all those things to be settled. . . ."

"What things?"

"Why, why—the reception and—all the plans and—Emily and Clare and . . . Oh, Kirk, my wedding dress!"

Kirk said, "Why take that ring off? It's yours. . . ."

"But not now! I mean, isn't it supposed to be bad luck? Wearing your wedding ring before . . ."

There was a little silence. Then Kirk said slowly, "There's no such thing as luck. A man makes his own luck, his own fortune, his own failure. I've made my good luck. I intend to continue to make it. I can do anything I have to do. . . . Is Josh one of the things to be settled?"

It flashed out unexpectedly, as Kirk's questions so often did, with the swift precision of a knife. The ring wasn't too tight; it fit perfectly, yet it wouldn't budge. Her hand was unsteady. But there was nothing unsteady, nothing indecisive about her reply, for that was already firmly established. "No," she said.

It didn't satisfy Kirk. "Look at me, Maggy."

She looked up, and his eyes were so very clear and light that they seemed to pierce straight to every thought, every fleeting—and guilty—impulse she had ever had. He said, "Did Josh come to Milrock intending to try to break up our marriage?"

"Oh, no!" she cried. "He came to Milrock because . . ." With dismay she heard her own words and stopped in full flight, on the very verge of telling Kirk exactly why Josh had come.

She had made a decision about that, too, and it had seemed to be a decision which was fair to Josh and fair to Kirk.

And besides, she thought unexpectedly, if she told Kirk that Josh had come to Milrock to investigate the Beall Company, it would be like touching off a powder keg— worse, a whole train packed with ammunition.

Something flickered in Kirk's gray eyes. "Go on. Why did Josh come to Milrock?"

Her thoughts scurried like frightened chickens at the shadow of a hawk. She had not promised Josh anything. Certainly her first loyalty lay toward Kirk. But Josh would find nothing fraudulent. She said, "Why shouldn't he come to Milrock? It's his home. Kirk, believe me, his coming here had nothing to do with me."

It was the literal truth, if not the entire truth. And if Kirk had only known it, she thought, it was a declaration of her faith in him. She gave a final tug to the ring and it came off. Kirk said, "What exactly did Josh say to you last night when he took you up to the arbor?"

153

She wasn't afraid, she couldn't be afraid of Kirk, but nevertheless her words stumbled. "Why, he—he talked—about George. . . ."

"Don't try to lie to me, Maggy," Kirk said.

Her eyes caught a flicker of motion beyond Kirk. She looked and it was Josh, sauntering along, yet approaching rather quickly, too. He looked as if he had all the time in the world, as if he had nothing on his mind, no purpose, no intent whatever, and Maggy had an inexplicable impulse to move between him and Kirk.

Josh reached them, said, "A fine rehearsal. I'm glad I happened to drop in and watch . . ." and got no further, for Kirk's fist shot out with all the strength of his shoulder behind it and caught Josh squarely on the chin.

Josh gave a kind of gasp and slid down to the floor, quite gently, very neatly; it was like a moving picture turned to slow motion.

Kirk looked down at Josh and flexed his hand as if the fingers hurt. Inside the church Dr. Norris' voice boomed out clearly, ". . . better be at the church at least half an hour, certainly fifteen minutes, before the ceremony."

They hadn't seen it, they hadn't heard it, Maggy thought with stricken astonishment. Josh had fallen just inside the vestibule, out of sight of the little group at the altar railing. She started toward Josh, and Kirk said, "He's all right."

Josh made a motion to get up, and Kirk himself leaned over, put his hand under Josh's arm and helped him to his feet. Josh dusted off his coat and touched his chin where a red blotch was spreading. He looked at Kirk with an odd little smile which wasn't a smile at all. "What exactly was that for?"

"To teach you to stay away from Maggy." There was a white line around Kirk's mouth, but his voice was perfectly low and controlled. The fuse was burning, however; the powder keg was about to explode, the ammunition train was going to go up, the whole place would rock with it. All of Milrock would rock with it.

It didn't. Josh rubbed his chin meditatively, eyed Kirk remotely, as if Kirk were some object which had to be brought into view by a telescope, and said, "There's an interesting violence in you, Kirk—well, this hardly seems the time and place. Shall we go outside and finish it off?"

Josh was taller than Kirk and looked, somehow, assured and certain of himself. Kirk, however, subtly and instantly took command of the situation.

"I've made allowances," Kirk said forthrightly. "I've tried to be fair, I think I have been fair. You owe me an apology, you can skip that. You owe Maggy an apology."

"Oh, I don't think I've insulted Maggy," Josh said.

"You understand what I'm trying to say."

"Go ahead and tell me. I'm interested."

"Oh, Josh, *don't!*" Maggy gave a swift look down at the group at the altar. Emily was shaking hands with the minister. Alroy was already starting up the aisle, and there was something inquisitive about his narrowed eyes. He began to walk faster.

Suddenly Kirk's winning, candid smile flashed over his face. "I'm sorry. Really sorry, Josh. I shouldn't have done that. I lost my temper."

"You did rather. Sure you don't want to finish it off?"

"Sure," Kirk said, and laughed.

The tension in Maggy collapsed with a merciful release. With that one rueful, friendly little laugh Kirk had put the whole thing in its right perspective. Besides, he had been in the right, she thought. She was to be his wife and Josh knew it. Josh was in the wrong.

The trouble was that Josh did not seem to know that. He said, "You're really very smart, Kirk." This time there was not the faintest edge of irony in his voice.

But again Kirk did exactly the right, the straightforward and candid thing. "Not so smart," he said, laughing. "I don't know what got into me."

But Maggy knew; she had evaded, she had tried to conceal the things Josh had told her, and Kirk had sensed it.

Kirk said, "Forget it, will you, Josh? I damn near started a scandal. Right here in the church, over nothing. I'm too happy a man to want to quarrel with anybody, certainly not you."

And she loved Kirk, she loved Kirk more than ever, Maggy thought with pride. She caught the flash of a skeptical, too-perceptive light in Josh's hazel eyes and looked away. Her hand was clenched hard around her wedding ring. She held it out toward Kirk and the ring glittered in beauty, on her reddened palm. Alroy came to them and said, "Anything wrong?"

"Wrong?" Kirk said. "What on earth should there be wrong?"

"Well, I thought—I mean you looked . . ." Alroy stopped.

His attention was diverted as Maggy put the wedding ring into Kirk's hand. Alroy watched greedily. Kirk replaced the ring in its velvet box.

Josh saw it, too. She wished obscurely that he hadn't. She hadn't intended to flaunt that lovely, costly wedding ring before Josh.

The others were nearing them. Mrs. Elwell, the expert on weddings, materialized beside Kirk, saying earnestly,

"You must remember to get to the altar before your sister starts down the aisle. Now, start from the vestry with the music, the best way is to count . . ."

Kirk listened with courteous attention. Clare said that Alroy was going back to the works in Kirk's car and Kirk would ride home with them in her car.

By the time they came out of the church, Josh had disappeared. The fog seemed heavier; it weighed down the tall oaks around the church so that they bent as if to watch the wedding party. It was warm, though; there was a breathless, oppressive quality in the air and it was very still. "A good rain would clear this up," Kirk said as they got into Clare's little car.

"Just so it doesn't rain tomorrow," Clare said, and adjusted herself behind the wheel. Maggy sat between them.

It would have been better, she thought, far better not to try to evade Kirk's questions; he had a right to ask them, and she owed him direct and truthful answers. He had let his smoldering anger flare out at Josh but on the other hand, he had instantly controlled himself, and Josh, too, with poise and a candid and friendly apology. She needn't have been afraid of powder kegs or anything. Kirk knew, he always knew, how to control any situation. And, she thought again, Kirk was in the right.

Clare guided the car around a truck which loomed up out of the fog and said, "It's funny—seems as if the wedding is over and you are already married. . . . Oh." She slowed down. "There's a light in Ralph's office. I wonder if they've found him."

The car was directly opposite the white clapboard house on Main Street. Between the arching oaks that lined the street, Maggy could see the shingle beside the open

157

door: Ralph Hewitt, Attorney-At-Law. There was a wide window, lighted as Clare had said, showing a desk; a typewriter and other office equipment caught metallic highlights. A girl in a brown dress, wearing spectacles, seemed to be talking to someone who was just out of sight. Clare stopped the car. A man in the uniform of a state trooper came into view and seemed to speak to the girl.

Clare said, "That's the Hinckley girl. She works for Ralph. At least she goes to his office about twice a week, transcribes from records whatever dictation he has done, posts his books and writes out his bills. Not many bills, I imagine."

Kirk bent to look past Maggy. "There's Josh, too."

It was Josh. There was a glimpse of a sandy head and part of a dark coat. Clare looked at Kirk. "Shall we ask if they've found Ralph?"

"I will." Kirk got out of the car. He strode lightly around it, across the strip of grass and in through the open door. Clare watched, Maggy watched; it was like a scene in the theatre. The girl looked up as Kirk entered, and apparently spoke to him. The policeman spoke with, what seemed even at that distance, a suggestion of deference in his manner. They talked a little; the policeman shook his head. Then the girl said something. Josh still remained almost out of sight, although Maggy thought he reached for a cigarette. She was sure when she saw the little flare of a match. The policeman nodded at Kirk deferentially again and Kirk came out.

He walked quickly, swinging along with grace and ease as always; his face, though, was grave. Clare said from the open window, "Have they found him?"

Kirk shook his head, went around the car and got in beside Maggy again. "Nothing yet, he said."

Clare started the car. "What was the state trooper doing in Ralph's office?"

"He said people were saying that Ralph may have drowned himself intentionally. Everybody knows he was an expert swimmer. He was asking the Hinckley girl if she knew any reason for suicide. Pressing debts, depression, anything like that."

"Did the girl know anything?"

"Well, Ralph was always over his ears in debt. Everybody knew it. I don't think there was anything new. He asked me if I thought Ralph could have turned the canoe over purposely. He could have, of course. There was a kind of jolt—something. I don't know what. It happened too fast."

Clare turned the corner onto the road that went to the Beall place. "Wasn't that Josh Mason in there, too?"

Kirk nodded. "He saw the light and stopped to inquire about Ralph."

That's not why he stopped, Maggy thought. He wanted to know why the state trooper was there. She felt an obscure kind of waver and unsteadiness, as if the car had struck a bump on the smoothly paved road.

Clare said after a while, "If Ralph capsized the canoe on purpose—why that would be murder, Kirk. He knew you can't swim! And Lydia was there, too!"

"If Ralph was in a state of mind for suicide he wouldn't stop to think of me or Lydia. But honestly I don't think it was intentional. He may have made some clumsy move that capsized us, but—no, I don't think he meant suicide. As a matter of fact, I don't think he could have stopped himself from swimming. It would have been instinctive with Ralph."

"Cramps then," Clare said. "Or the current was too

strong. Well, you never know really about a drowning accident. We'd better get on home to lunch."

The car went faster, too fast really on the slippery pavement. Clare was frowning, her hands tense on the wheel. Maggy thought, Josh hasn't given up—and I'm going to warn Kirk.

Lunch, hurriedly assembled by Mrs. Elwell and Mildred, was waiting for them. It was haphazard, interrupted by the arrival of the express truck with more wedding gifts, the caterer on the telephone asking for the latest count of guests who had accepted, and the Milrock Inn wanting to know exactly how many reservations to make for guests who were staying over for the night. Emily bustled about, a plate of salad in her hand. Kirk got on the telephone to ask Dr. Mason if he would give Maggy away, and failed to reach him. Clare snatched the telephone from Kirk to inquire of the dressmaker whether or not her dress had been shortened. Emily lost some scissors for opening packages and told Maggy she must pack. Mildred came in to say that the police had come while they were at rehearsal. "They brought back the canoe," she said, "and one of the paddles. I didn't know what to tell them to do, so they tied the canoe up at the landing."

Mrs. Elwell came in with the coffee. "That'll do, Mildred," she said repressively. Emily asked Clare what she had done with the lists.

"I haven't the faintest idea," Clare said, took the scissors she had found and ripped brown wrapping paper noisily from a large cardboard box.

Kirk poured coffee for Maggy and for himself. "Let's take this to my study," he said, and led the way. "Quieter in here. Clare's in one of her moods. I know the signs." He closed the door. He cleared a space on the table that stood before the deep sofa; its cushions were covered with red leather and looked worn. The room itself was rather gloomy, paneled with dark oak as was the hall; there were old-fashioned glass-covered bookcases. A long desk stood before the windows. Kirk turned on the green-shaded desk lamp, which spread a pool of light upon papers, note pads, his dictating machine, a telephone. He did much of his work there; it was like a small and concentrated office. Maggy sat on the sofa and wondered how many evenings she and Kirk would spend in that room, Kirk working at the desk while she watched or read.

"You're looking very serious," Kirk said. "It's the wedding that upset Clare a little, I expect. Thinking of her own marriage, you see. She should never have married Alroy. I've done everything I can for him but he resents it, naturally I suppose. However, he owes Clare loyalty at least."

Maggy's mind went back to her talk with Clare the night before, and Lydia's divorce. There was another man, Clare had said; there's always another man. "What do you mean about Alroy?"

"Oh, nothing really. He's got an eye for an attractive woman."

"Do you mean anyone in particular?"

Kirk gave her one glance. His eyes were as clear and hard as diamonds. "Lydia? I don't know. I'll tell you the truth. When Josh brought up the question of murder, I did just—well, think of Alroy. You see, Lydia was a very determined woman. She was also extremely—oh, conventional. If Alroy had made a few passes at her—she was a beauty in her way and he may have done just that—Lydia might have taken it very seriously and hopped off to get a divorce, intending to come back and make Alroy marry her. It would have scared Alroy out of his not-too-bright wits. His job depends upon me. He wouldn't want to give up everything that Clare and I have made possible for him. On the other hand, Lydia would certainly have known that if Alroy made a move to get Clare to divorce him so he could marry Lydia, I'd have kicked him out. Lydia wasn't likely to give up a good steady living from George and take on Alroy with no money and no prospects. So, unless I've overlooked something, that idea is out entirely."

He put his coffee cup down and leaned against the edge of the desk. "Besides, I couldn't, and I can't now, seriously consider the faintest possibility of murder. Naturally, though, after an accusation like that, I did some thinking."

"Alroy rescued Lydia. At least he helped."

"Yes, I thought that, too. It's true that Lydia might have got it into her head that Alroy was in fact trying to— oh, push her under the water or something like that. But that is really not reasonable. Besides, some of you would have seen it. I've tried to look at it from Josh's point of view last night. But while Alroy was in the house when Lydia died, that doesn't make it murder or Alroy a murderer. George seems to have been wandering about, too— jealous husbands have murdered their wives before now, but I can't see George killing Lydia. I was in the canoe when it went over. Or when, just possibly, Ralph turned it over. If I hadn't managed to get hold of the canoe, I'd have been drowned. I really wouldn't have taken a chance of drowning, even if I had wanted to murder Lydia—as really, Maggy, I didn't! I was in the house, too, when Lydia died, but . . ." He shook his head thoughtfully. "Oh, it's absurd really. Dr. Mason settled that last night— I lost my temper a bit with Josh this morning. Maybe that's natural though. I am as possessive as the next man."

He walked over to the sofa. "There's no reason to bother about Josh. He took it rather well this morning. Probably knew he deserved it, as a matter of fact."

Now was the time to tell Kirk exactly what Josh still believed. And now was the time to tell Kirk why Josh had come to Milrock.

She wasn't afraid of Kirk, she wasn't afraid at all. She was trusting her entire future life to him. All the same, she had to steel herself.

She swallowed hard. "Kirk, Josh hasn't given up at all."

Kirk's face didn't change. There was not the slightest flicker in his eyes. She knotted her fingers together and plunged on. "That's what he said to me last night, up at the arbor. I ought to have told you right away this morning when you asked me what Josh had said."

"Why didn't you?" Kirk said softly.

"I didn't want—a quarrel or—and then, you see, Kirk . . ." She had to tell Kirk immediately, that instant, the reason for Josh's coming to Milrock and she couldn't. Her throat seemed to close.

"Well," Kirk said, watching her.

She pushed herself up, out of the sofa; the leather arms felt chill and clammy. She walked to the window and knew that Kirk was waiting and watching her. It was her clear duty to tell Kirk; her first loyalty was to Kirk.

So she ought not to feel that she was cutting the ground from under Josh's feet. She ought to have none of this choking sense of failure to keep some trust. She hadn't promised Josh not to tell Kirk, she hadn't promised him anything.

She had listened to him. That in itself was a kind of implicit promise. No, it wasn't, she told herself. He'd made her listen. And suddenly she was appalled at the strength

163

of the struggle going on within her. There should be no conflict at all.

She turned around and faced Kirk, who stood perfectly still beside the sofa. There was a tiny wrinkle between his eyebrows. She forced out the words, quickly, before anything within herself could stop her.

"The truth is, Josh was sent here to investigate the Company—I mean, your financial statement."

"I see," Kirk said.

Was he surprised, or had he already guessed it? There was no way to know. "It's unofficial." She hurried on. "He didn't want you to know."

"Well, that's all right." The tiny line smoothed itself out. Maggy took a quick, thankful breath. Kirk said evenly, "We've had a spectacular growth. Probably somebody in the firm he works for has some questions in spite of our accountants' statement. Let Josh investigate. He can see anything he wants to see. He'll not find anything wrong." He laughed shortly. "Maggy, was that why you looked so worried? Couldn't you have had a little more faith in me?"

She was intensely relieved. She ought to have known that Kirk's reaction would be sensible and straightforward.

Now that she had started, though, she had to finish. "And then he said that I am a witness. He still believes that Lydia was murdered. He said there couldn't ever be a proven case of murder without me. And I *am* a witness in that sense. I mean, I couldn't possibly swear that there was not a flush in Lydia's face when I found her. The more I think of it," she said miserably, "the more certain I am that there was."

Clare opened the door and came in. "George is here."

George Clowe came in. He came slowly, as if he were

drugged or half asleep. His plump face was splotched unhealthily with red as it had been the day before when he was drinking. There were purple hollows below his eyes. He was dressed, though, very precisely, very neatly, in a dark summer suit with a black tie.

Kirk started toward him, his hand out. Clare came in, too, and closed the door behind her. "George," she said, in a strained, harsh voice. "Why did Lydia divorce you? Was there another man?"

George turned slowly; he looked at her as if he didn't see her. "That's what Josh asked me this morning. That's why I came here."

FIFTEEN

Kirk lifted a heavy brass ash tray from the desk and slammed it down with a crash that seemed to rock the room. George winced and stared. Clare's hands twisted so hard together it must have hurt, Maggy thought absently, shaken, too, as if the ash tray had crashed against her own ears. Kirk himself seemed surprised; he moved the ash tray very softly to the center of the desk. Then he walked around it and took up the telephone.

Clare's eyes flashed. She ran across to the desk and seized the telephone. "No . . ."

For a moment Kirk and Clare were like a picture, caught and fixed in a moment of intense struggle. George said dully, "What are you doing, Kirk?"

Clare answered. "He's phoning the police."

"Why?" George said.

Kirk still held the telephone, with Clare's hands pressing down upon his own. He said evenly, "I have to, George. I'm going to have a full-scale investigation into Lydia's death—Ralph's death—all of it."

George blinked. He looked stunned and still half asleep. Obviously, he did not take in any meaning of Kirk's words. "Why?" he said again.

"Because of that damn fool Josh Mason."

Clare's hands relaxed. "You can't do that, Kirk. Scandal, newspapers—right now before the wedding!"

Maggy's knees were shaking. She went across to the sofa and sat down again, thankful for its support, thankful for Clare's intervention—and yet obscurely troubled by it, too.

If there was ever the slightest question of murder, anywhere, at any time, wasn't it better to answer it? Dr. Mason had answered it. Dr. Mason *could* have been mistaken.

George said, "But what do you mean? I don't understand. Did you say an investigation?"

Josh had not talked to George of murder then, Maggy thought. But Clare knew. She tugged at George's arm. "Never mind that. Listen, George. Why did Lydia divorce you?"

"Why, because—because she said she wasn't happy. She said our marriage wasn't . . ." George rubbed his eyes. "I don't know really, Clare. I didn't understand it. Lydia was strong for ideals and—and all that."

Clare nodded once. "I thought she'd put it on a high plane," she said, and then, like Kirk, dived straight for the core, a definite, specific fact. "Have you looked through her things, George, at the house? Her letters?"

"Yes," George said simply. "Yes, I did. I was at the house—our house—this morning. Josh came and he asked that, too. He asked, why did Lydia divorce me and—was there another man? I told him there wasn't any man. I tried to explain Lydia, she was too fine, too idealistic and—there wasn't any other man. I told Josh that but—I don't know—after he'd gone I . . ." The red splotches on his face deepened. He said as if ashamed, "I looked. I searched all through her baggage. I hunted all through the house—everywhere, desk, writing table, everywhere. There wasn't anything—I mean, no letters, no special sort of letters, that is . . ."

"Love letters," Clare said definitely. "How about a diary?"

"Lydia? No."

Clare said, "Cables? Messages?"

George shook his head. "Lydia was always very neat, you know. Orderly. I hated to go searching through her things like that. There were things—dresses and things she had worn. I'd seen her wear them."

"Here." Clare took Maggy's forgotten cup of coffee with a swoop. She put it in George's hand. "Drink that."

"But then," George said, "I got to thinking. I couldn't get it out of my head. You see, I gave Lydia everything she wanted—that is, everything I could give her. I have done . . ." He stared at the rug. "I would have done anything for Lydia. So I couldn't really understand why she wanted a divorce. But maybe she was afraid to tell me. Maybe it was somebody—somebody I know. Somebody— you know. I came to ask you. I've got to know."

Clare gave her thick black hair a swing backward away from her face and over her shoulders. She came to the sofa, her yellow skirt swirling upward, and sat down beside Maggy in an oddly defensive way, almost as if Maggy or Clare or both of them required protection. She said, "I've got to know, too."

George said, "I was busy all this year, extra busy, at the works. Nights . . ." His voice trailed away. He seemed to look back over time. Finally he sighed. "I'm sorry, Clare. But was it Alroy?"

Clare stiffened. "No! At least—how could it have been Alroy?"

The lawyer in George was slowly beginning to arouse. He eyed Clare with a glimmer of his usual shrewdness.

"You thought of that, too. You aren't sure. That's why you said you had to know."

Kirk came around to the front of the desk and sat on the edge of it. "George, do you mean to say that Josh came to see you and just out of the blue asked you whether or not Lydia left you for another man? Why didn't you kick him out?"

George sighed. "I never thought of it. I wasn't myself. For one thing, I had a hangover. And then Lydia . . ."

"But the impertinence! The insulting . . ."

"Oh, no," George said simply. "Josh was really very nice about it. He seemed to feel sorry for me."

Clare leaned forward; her sharp strong profile was outlined against the light from the desk. "George," she said softly, "how well did Josh know Lydia?"

George was more like himself; his eyes narrowed instantly. "She didn't know him at all—or at least only very casually. Besides, he's been away for two years. . . ."

Clare interrupted. "And Lydia got her divorce so she'd be free at exactly the time Josh got out of the service and came home!"

Maggy rose as if something had shot her up out of the deep sofa. "No! It wasn't Josh! It wasn't Josh . . ." she cried and stopped, for George's eyes were shrewd now and intent, Clare and Kirk were watching her, too, looking exactly alike with their clear gray gaze.

But she was sure that Clare, or one of them, was about to say that if Lydia was murdered Josh might have murdered her. Josh had struck her there in the river; all of them had seen it. Maggy's thoughts flashed on. They could say—couldn't they?—that Josh raised the cry of murder because he hoped to cover himself by accusing someone else.

169

She had to break the strained silence with all of them, George and Clare and Kirk, looking at her, fixed and startled as if they saw Maggy as a new person, somebody they had never seen before. She turned to George. "You were here last night. You went up to the arbor. You took a blanket and then you came back to the house and found the candle on the terrace. You lighted it and came into the house for whiskey. Did you see anything or—or anyone . . ." She intended to say: anyone who might have murdered Lydia. George's eyes were so surprised and troubled she couldn't say it, point-blank like that in the face of his grief.

Clare caught her breath sharply. Kirk didn't move and Maggy felt that his eyes registered every motion of her lips, the very beat of her pulse, and made an indelible record of them.

George said, "Why yes." He turned to Kirk. "I didn't tell you and Alroy last night. I mean when you heard me start the car and came out to tell me about Lydia. I was— I told you I wasn't myself. The fact is, I already knew that Lydia was dead."

Kirk didn't look at him; he didn't look away from Maggy. George went on. "I guess I had passed out. I woke up in Alroy's room—it was nearly dark. I was still very fuzzy. I knew Lydia was here in the house and she wouldn't want me to stay here. But I wasn't in a condition to drive, either. It seemed a good idea to go up to the arbor and sleep it off. Out of the house, you see, so as not to upset Lydia. So I got a blanket and went up to the arbor. I slept for a long time. When I woke up, I was cold. I came back to the house. I was going to get another drink. I had matches and I saw a candle on the balustrade and lighted it.

I tried the door of the living room and it was open. I came in and got a bottle of whiskey out of the dining room."

Kirk interrupted. "Did you see Lydia then?"

George waited a second, then the breath went out of him. "Yes. I thought, I don't know why, but I thought that if I went to her then and talked to her—I was going to tell her that I tried to rescue her and—well, I just thought that she might listen and we might effect a reconciliation." The phrase sounded curiously prim and was precisely the phrase that suited George. "I'd have done anything to get her back, you know. Nothing was too much if Lydia . . ."

"You went to her room?" Kirk asked.

"I—yes," George said. He seemed to try to divert Kirk's questions. "I guess I took your sleeping capsules, too, Maggy. At least I got them from your room. I saw your wedding dress. That was in the evening, when I left Alroy's room and started to the arbor. The door to your room was open and I—I wasn't really drunk then, you understand, but still I wasn't myself—I saw the dress and—I don't know, I just stopped to stare at it. And there on the table by the door there was a bottle of sleeping capsules and I thought I'd take them with me so as to get some sleep. I tell you I wasn't myself. . . ."

"What did you do with the capsules?" Kirk asked.

"What did I . . . ?" George stared at the rug. Finally he looked up at Kirk. "I put the bottle in my pocket and went up to the arbor. I didn't take any capsules. Then later . . ."

"Later, did you give any to Lydia?"

"No." George's eyes were blank and dull. "No, she was dead."

"George!" Clare said on a sharp breath.

171

Kirk put up his hand as if to stop her. George said as if seizing any tangent, "Oh, yes—you asked me about the bottle of capsules, Kirk. I took it out of my pocket—it was in Lydia's room. I remember thinking that she couldn't really be dead. And that I ought to give her something or do something, or maybe I took out the bottle, you know, without knowing it, but I think I put it down somewhere."

"George," Kirk said. "Are you sure that Lydia was dead then?"

"Yes," George said dully.

There was a long silence. Then Kirk said, "So you didn't get to talk to her at all?"

"No. She was dead. Face down in the pillow. Wouldn't speak to me or—you know, I was stunned. I didn't know what I was doing. I remember there was some water there in the thermos. I thought of giving Lydia some water or putting some on her face or—but of course I knew she was dead. I could tell that. All at once I wasn't drunk any more. That happens, you know."

He went off on another tangent which offered escape from the memory of Lydia. "A fellow dead drunk gets a shock, everything clears up. Anyway, it cleared up then. I felt her pulse and waited. I pulled up the sheet. It was all twisted and wrinkled. She wouldn't have liked that. So I pulled up the sheet so it was neat and—then I came out and all at once it was as if I was dead drunk again. I didn't want to see anybody or talk to anybody or—somehow I got downstairs and there was the whiskey and the candle right where I'd left them on the bottom step. I picked them up—somehow it seemed important—I don't know. I remember getting out the terrace door and trying to be quiet. I put the candle down on the balustrade and—yes, I think I blew out the flame."

She had missed him then, Maggy thought, by only a few moments. Could she have so nearly met murder, face to face?

George went on. "The next thing I knew I'd been in the arbor a long time. Drinking straight from the bottle." He pulled himself up with a suggestion of his customary primness. "I don't drink much as a rule."

There was another long silence in the room. Finally, Kirk said, "What did you do then?"

George's slight air of dignity collapsed. "I don't know. I thought somebody was coming to the arbor. I thought I heard somebody along the path. I left the arbor. I guess I wandered on over the hillside. I sat down for a while, leaned against a tree. After a long time I thought somebody called me and I didn't want to see anybody. So I went down to the road. Then I thought about the car and I came back up the drive to the house. I was starting my car when somebody shouted at me. Alroy began to tell me about Lydia. You told me, too."

Maggy said suddenly, "Did you see Lydia's face?"

"Yes," George said, and unexpectedly, dreadfully, dropped the cup of coffee and put his hands over his face. The coffee splashed, the cup rolled a little across the rug and didn't break.

The break—the small crack—was in the wall of Maggy's conviction that Josh was wrong, that Lydia had not been murdered, that there was no such thing as murder in the night in the house, anywhere. Her voice came out tense as a strung wire. "George, was her face flushed? Was it dark red . . . ?"

"Don't," George said from behind his hands. "I can't bear it. . . ."

It was true, then; George had answered the question she could not answer. She felt queerly cold.

Kirk went to George and put his hand on George's shoulder.

"I could see that you and Alroy were trying to make it easy for me," George said. "Trying to soften it. I just listened while you told me that Lydia was dead. I'd had a lot of whiskey—that and shock and—none of it seemed real."

"All right, George, all right. Did you tell Josh all this?"

"No." George dropped his hands and looked up at Kirk. "I told you—we talked of other things for the most part."

"What things?"

"Why—the business, the stock issue, all that . . ."

Kirk interrupted. "I should tell you. Josh was sent here to investigate us."

"Us?" George said blankly.

"The Company. Our financial statements. Everything."

George is in it, too; Josh had said that, Maggy thought, and tried to rein in her memory, but it galloped on—*if there's any funny business at the works, George is in it, too.* She couldn't keep from watching either of the men. Was there a flash of intelligence between George and Kirk?

There was not. Or if there was, it was too swift for her to see. George said, "Oh, well—that's to be expected. Except . . ." He looked puzzled. "I don't see why they'd send Josh."

"It's not important," Kirk said. "Just tell him anything he wants to know."

"Yes—yes, of course." There was, though, still a look of puzzled question in George's face lifted up toward Kirk. "Kirk—when I came in just now you went to the phone. You said you were going to call the police. I didn't quite take it in. I didn't see . . ." He pulled himself up out of the chair and said directly, "Why were you going to call the police? You said something about an investigation. About Lydia's death and Ralph's death. What did you mean?"

"That's not important, either," Kirk said. "We'll talk about it later."

But George's normal shrewdness had returned. "Investigation and police. Do you mean . . ."

Clare said, "Josh says that Lydia was murdered."

George turned so slowly that an immense time seemed to pass before he spoke. The red patches in his face drained away slowly, too. "Josh didn't say that to me! Dr. Mason said it was a heart attack. What do you mean—murder . . . ?"

Clare said, "You saw Lydia. Josh thinks she was smothered. A pillow over her face."

Suddenly red flooded back into George's face. His eyes were suffused and crimson; his hands trembled, his whole body shook. He shouted, "If anybody killed her I'll kill him. I'll do anything, nothing will stop me—I'll kill him. . . ."

"George—George," Kirk cried.

George spluttered and choked and tore at his collar.

Clare said, "He's going to have a stroke." She flashed up and across to George. "Stop it, George. Take it easy. . . ."

She turned to Kirk, and Kirk said, "There's nothing to it. Lydia was not murdered. Now, believe me, listen to me."

"You've got to answer me! You've got to tell me! You can't stop me. . . ."

"Come with me, George, come with me," Clare put her hands on George's arm. She led him toward the door, talking soothingly as if to a child. "Now be quiet, take it easy. I'll explain everything. You'd better lie down for a minute. Come on. You've had a terrible shock, I'll tell you everything, but you've got to calm down now."

She had him out the door and into the hall. She leaned back to close the door behind them. Maggy stood like a stone.

The crack in her wall of disbelief had widened to an enormous, fatal crevasse. She stood and watched the flood of suspicion that poured through it.

Kirk said, "Clare knows all about Josh's talk of murder?"

Maggy replied, and was astonished in some distant corner of her consciousness to hear her own voice, perfectly quiet and perfectly cool. "Alroy heard us talking last night. He told Clare."

"She was afraid Alroy killed Lydia." He said it flatly, a mere statement of fact.

"Yes—I suppose so."

"George . . ." Kirk walked to the window and back, his head bent. "No," he said finally. "I can't believe George would kill Lydia. Yet he was drunk, by his own admission. He was the injured husband—if Alroy *was* the cause of their divorce. Clare hated Lydia. I never knew why. But Clare—no, no! Clare wouldn't have—no woman could have put that pillow over Lydia's head. . . ."

"No," Maggy cried. "It couldn't have been Clare!"

"It wasn't murder! We're letting what George told us confuse us. . . ."

"You know it was murder."

"George was drunk. . . ."

"The police have to know," Maggy said.

Kirk came to her. "Listen, Maggy. There is no real evidence of murder. If I call the police and tell them all this, I can do a great deal of harm. Do you think they would believe George's story?" He stopped. He looked down at her for a long moment. Something flickered at last in his eyes, like the small click of a camera. She had a fantastic notion that he had perceived and put down forever, in black and white like a photograph, some quality in her which she could never change or erase.

Then very deliberately he put his arms around her and drew her close to him. He held her as if he never meant to let her go, or as if he himself were going away on a long trip and was saying farewell. But by this time tomorrow he would be her husband—to have and to hold from this day forward. He put his hand around her face, cupping it, and then down along her throat exploringly. The room around her seemed to dissolve. She was lost and breathless.

He released her. "I can do anything I have to do," he said. "I'll see to George." He went out of the room without looking back.

She sank down into the sofa. Her knees were shaking again.

There wasn't a sound in the house anywhere. You are a witness, Josh had said; there is no murder case without you. She was halfway to the door before she knew that she was going to the arbor and why.

She went into the hall. As she did so, Mrs. Elwell hurried past and opened the front door. Two men came in carrying huge white cardboard boxes. "Is that the wedding cake?" Mrs. Elwell said. "Take it back to the pantry. Careful now . . ."

Mrs. Elwell led the way. The two men wore blue uniforms with jaunty triangles on their jackets outlining the words Jensen Catering Service. They carried the white boxes carefully, as if they were fragile. It was her wedding cake in its several layers, later to be put together. She passed it and the men.

She went out onto the terrace. The flagstones were shining and wet. The chairs were damp and uninviting. The roses hung sodden and heavy, their bright crimson edged with purple. There was no sky; only a thick, pearly gray which pressed down upon the house, the roses, the trees, everything. Wraiths of fog twisted among the willows and shut off even the silvery gleams from the river. She went down the steps and across the lawn and into the path to the arbor. The windows of the house surveyed her from their draperies of ivy, but if anyone saw her enter the path she did not know it.

SIXTEEN

In the daylight it was simply a path that turned now and again through trees and undergrowth and climbed steeply upward. It bore no witness of her headlong flight down it during the night. She came out quite soon really upon the open space where the arbor stood. Nothing about it was changed.

There was the little rocky space above the river, there were the encircling greens of trees and vines, laurels and more brambles, all of them looking dreary and wet that foggy day. There was the arbor; she went to the entrance and looked in. The blanket lay crumpled as she had dropped it. The bottle of whiskey stood beside a rustic chair. The two chairs were still pushed close together, as they had been the night before. Josh had sat just there, so close to her she could feel his arm pressing against her own. A loop of roses peered into the arbor over her shoulder. The roses were faded, as if they had been drained of their blood red color.

If anyone had overheard their conversation and had resolved to make an end to a dangerous witness—me, Maggy thought—then he must have stood somewhere near the arbor. George?

George had been, by his own confession, roaming through the woods on the hillside, drunk and confused. Oh yes, it might have been George.

If he had murdered Lydia, would he have made so dangerous a confession? Would he have admitted having gone to her room? George was shrewd and perhaps he was wily. What about the rock which had bounced down and down to the river?

That day there were no distant hills, not even the glimmer of the river. The fog was so heavy that she could barely see the darker moving grays of the river directly below. Farther out, only a little farther out, the river merged completely with the fog. She went to the edge of the lookout point and looked down the slope.

It was not as steep as it had seemed the night before in the darkness and in fear. It was irregular and there were clumps of tough and stubborn growth all the way down. In the daytime, even if she made a misstep and plunged over the little lip of rocks, she could easily save herself. At night, though, it wouldn't have been so easy. What about the rock? Rocks do dislodge themselves. Certainly people don't stand in the dark and pelt other people with rocks. Besides, she was not a good target; she could have been no more fully visible to anyone who might have stood there near her in the darkness, than that person—if there was such a person—had been visible to her.

No, that was wrong. She had worn a white dressing gown. It might have loomed up, dimly perhaps, but outlining the target, herself. But still it would have been a random, hit-or-miss attack, more likely to miss, certain only to frighten her.

A rock, though, can be put to other uses. A rock, say, can be seized upon as a weapon, a hurried, extemporaneous sort of weapon, like a club. And then later who would know that the concussion, the deadly bruise, had not been caused in a fall down the slope or by some rock along the river banks. It would be an accident.

She didn't like venturing so close to the edge of the rocks even in the daylight, even when she was sure that she was alone, but she examined it inch by inch. She ranged farther, hunting for some mark, some clear little spot which showed less stain of time and weather, where a rock might have been dislodged—and found it. There was a shallow hollow, its outline preserved perfectly, scarcely more than a hand's breadth, but the soil was darker and damp, a few tiny white roots wound through it, white because of their lack of exposure to the sun. There were a hundred infinitesimal marks which showed that sometime, until quite lately—until last night—a rock had wedged itself down into the soil.

All right then, face it, she told herself. Someone dug out that rock, someone waited to get close to her, someone intended to smash the rock so hard against her temple that she could not have fought back, she'd have been unconscious, and then—nothing easier—push her over the ledge. She couldn't have saved herself, not then.

But she had saved herself instinctively. She had slid back into the shadow of the laurels, back and back so there was no longer the dim target of her white robe. So after waiting, whoever had stood there, that small rock in hand like a club, listened, waited, decided the quarry had escaped—tossed the rock away into the darkness, so by chance it fell into the river, and took a swift and silent way—where? Up along the wooded hillside? Or down through the woods to the house?

But that was attempted murder, she thought with a deep, inward shock of realization. She had come to the arbor to search out the very evidence she had found, yet

181

finding it was like a new and utterly stunning disclosure. It brought with it a kind of shock wave of terror.

She was alone, she was sure she was alone on the small promontory but she turned, cautiously, as if someone were watching. She moved back, too, from the edge of the rocks.

There was no one there, no one in the arbor, no one anywhere. The green vines masked the hillside behind the arbor. The thick clumps of laurels glistened with fog. The roses drooped soggily in faded red masses. "You could scream here until you were blue in the face and nothing but the roses would hear you."

Someone was coming down the hillside, behind the arbor. There was the snapping of twigs, the crash of footsteps through the shrubbery. Her impulse was to run for the path and the house. But Josh had come before, like that, that first day—sliding in the pine needles, catching at the arbor, standing out on the rocks to look at the river.

She waited a moment, unsure yet sure, too. And Josh came around the arbor. "Maggy! What's wrong?" He strode quickly across to her. He put his arm around her, supporting her.

"It's—you," she said.

"Of course, it's me. I came here hoping to see you. I didn't expect to find you right here though—I thought I'd go to the house and try to get hold of you. . . . You look terrified. What's wrong. . . . ?"

"Josh—could your father have been mistaken?"

"When he said Lydia wasn't murdered? Of course. Admitted it to me. Says cyanosis disappears very quickly, unless it's gas poisoning. Says if it *was* murder you found her within minutes, seconds almost."

"Does he think now that it was murder?"

No. But murder is nothing a doctor—any doctor—would ordinarily think of—or bring himself to accept without very definite suspicion. Besides, he knows them all too well. The Bealls—Lydia herself. He says in short that he could be mistaken but does not for a moment believe that he was mistaken. . . . Maggy, what's happened to you? Answer me."

"I think somebody tried to kill me. Last night . . ."

His arm tightened hard around her. Then he turned her to face him; his eyes were like swords, his mouth a hard line. "Tell me . . ."

She told him, in scattered, hurried phrases, but he seemed to understand. He left her and went to look at the patch of freshly exposed soil, where a small rock had lain. He looked down at the slope toward the river. He came back to her. "I shouldn't have left you here alone last night. But I had to find George if I could and put a flea in his ear. And I really didn't think it would happen so soon."

"It would happen . . . ?"

"An attempt to murder you," he said. "Are you sure you have no idea who it was?"

"It could have been George. George was here just now. And he said that he was in the house last night. He was in Lydia's room. He said she was dead, then."

"So he came here! I thought he would."

"You—planned that."

"George is the only lever, the only chance—I didn't tell him that I believe Lydia was murdered. I counted on—did anybody tell him that?"

"Clare told him."

"What did he say?"

"He was beside himself. He was berserk. He said he'd do anything, he'd kill anybody who hurt her. He could have killed her. He said—at least I'm sure he saw her face where it was discolored. And—Josh, Lydia *had* locked her door. She must have unlocked it herself but it was George who brought the capsules to her room. . . ."

"What's that?"

She told him quickly, as accurately as she could remember, everything George had said and everything that had been said to him.

"And," she finished, "Lydia wouldn't have unlocked the door for somebody she was afraid of. She might have unlocked it if George called to her."

"You said that you didn't hear or see George, then."

"I must have just missed him. Perhaps that was what woke me—when he went out the terrace door. If he didn't kill Lydia, he was certainly in her room minutes—your father said almost seconds—after she died."

"Well," Josh said after a moment. "That locked door of Lydia's isn't important—except it does seem to show that she was afraid. She may have unlocked it herself for some reason. But those are old locks and probably a dozen keys in the house fit them all. No—I don't think there's any provable evidence there, either."

"You said—in the house. A dozen keys—in the house."

He nodded, quickly, as if he had made up his mind.

"Come with me."

"What are you going to do?"

"It may not work. But I don't see any other way. Come with me, Maggy."

They went back down the path. They came out on the lawn and instead of going to the house, he marched her across the wet lawn in full view of all the windows which peered at them from their curtains of ivy. They came to

184

the flagstone path and then to the little landing, where Josh stopped. "Stay here. I'll be back in a minute."

He seemed to saunter again, slowly as he had along the aisle of the church, yet at the same time covered space very rapidly. He vanished in the direction of the garage.

The great loops and festoons of roses hanging over the backstops of the tennis court looked drained, too, and pale. Josh came back. He held something close against his side, concealed by his coat. "I thought I saw one in the garage. Now then, Maggy, I want you to do exactly as I say. Get into the canoe."

It lay below the landing, rocking gently. She held Josh's hand and stepped down into it. "Back there," Josh said. "Take the seat at the end."

A canoe can overbalance even in shallow water, even when secured by its painter to one of the brown weather-stained old pilings which supported the landing. She made her way carefully past the middle seat, back to the tiny seat where Lydia had sat. She sat down and linked her hands around her knees.

Josh got down into the canoe. He had some sort of tool with a red handle in his hand. She couldn't see what it was, for he slid it under the seat. Then he stepped up to the landing again. He took out cigarettes. "Now we wait," he said. "Want a cigarette, Maggy?"

She shook her head. Yesterday she had watched this canoe—only yesterday—floating along upside down after spilling its occupants into the deep current of the river. The paddle which the police had found and returned lay on the landing. They had even retrieved the orange-colored cushion which had bobbed along so gaily in the water, and it lay in the canoe. Josh saw it, too. He got down into the canoe again, took the cushion and tossed it

185

across the landing to the other side, where it fell in the
water with a subdued slap.

"Why did you do that?"

"It's a life preserver," Josh said. He glanced up toward
the house. His face instantly became alert and intent, and
at the same time without any expression at all.

Something terrible was going to happen. She waited for
it as she had waited and watched while the tiny crack of
her disbelief in murder had widened and let a whole flood
of suspicions pour down over her head, swamping her.

There was a sound beyond the curve of pines. She said
in a sharp whisper, "Somebody's coming along the path."

"Yes, I know," Josh said.

Alroy lounged into view. "Hello, Alroy," Josh said.

Alroy's big body looked slack and lazy, but his slaty
eyes were sharply inquisitive. "What are you doing
here?"

"Talking," Josh said. "I thought you were at the works."

"I was, but Clare phoned for me."

"How long have you been here?"

"Oh—half an hour or so. Why?"

"Were you by any chance up at the arbor?"

Alroy shot a suspicious glance at Josh. "Certainly not.
Why would I go up there? As a matter of fact, I've been
having a row with Clare." A sudden wave of crimson
surged into Alroy's face. "Women! You can't figure them.
I never so much as looked at Lydia. I didn't even like
Lydia! Why, if a man made a pass at Lydia she'd scream
for the police. Or wedding bells!"

"Did you make a pass?" Josh said coolly.

"Good heavens, no! But Clare—well, Clare questioned
me just now. It's your fault, Josh! If you hadn't gone
around talking about murder—oh, I heard you, all of you,

last night in the sewing room talking to your father. I had nothing to do with Lydia's divorce."

"Does Clare believe you?"

"Listen, Josh." Alroy's great fist doubled up. "You started all this, and you're wrong. I didn't kill Lydia, and Clare knows I didn't. There was nobody in the house who would have killed her. George was wandering around drunk, but he wouldn't have hurt Lydia, he'd have done anything for her. There were Kirk and Cousin Emily and Maggy and Clare herself. Clare's got a will of her own, sure, so has Kirk. They quarrel, but they stand together when the chips are down. But Clare wouldn't go in there and murder a woman, and Kirk's out of his head over Maggy. He didn't give a hoot for Lydia. My advice to you, Josh, is to shut up and get out," he said, whirled around and slouched back off the landing and along the path.

Josh said, thoughtfully, "Clare's in love with Alroy. She'd be jealous if she thought she had any reason to be. He's a big handsome lummox, but she likes him and he's hers." His hand, which had been absently turning the paddles, stilled.

Maggy heard the light leisurely pad of footsteps again along the path. The planks of the landing rattled softly, and Kirk came around the pines toward them. He had changed from the light business suit he had worn at rehearsal. He was wearing brown slacks and a jacket. He looked debonair, poised and handsome.

He had seen Maggy—he must have seen her—but he said, half laughing, to Josh, "What did you do to Alroy? I met him just now and he's like a bear with a sore head. Says he's going to throw you off the place."

"He's had some words with Clare."

187

"Oh. Yes, I know. She got it into her head that Alroy liked Lydia—a little too much."

"Did he?"

Kirk sobered. "Now look here, Josh. Let's not have any more of this talk of murder. Clare wouldn't have hurt Lydia. . . . I saw you coming across the lawn and I want to talk to you." The ease, the friendliness was back. "Why didn't you tell me that you came here to investigate our company?" he said with smiling reproach.

"Maggy told you," Josh said flatly.

"Why, of course. And very properly. But why didn't *you* tell me? I'll tell you anything you want to know. Glad to."

"Splendid," Josh said. "Sit down there, next to Maggy." Kirk looked startled. "In the canoe?"

"Why not? I've been wanting to talk to you about this." Kirk hesitated, glancing out at the sullen, cold river.

Josh said, "You're not afraid, are you?"

He held the paddle in a rather odd and awkward way, almost as if it were a club. Kirk did not see that. He still did not seem to see Maggy, either. He must have seen her, yet she had an extraordinary feeling that she had become invisible to him.

He stepped down into the canoe and Josh followed. The canoe wobbled. Josh untied the painter, swiftly, as Kirk was seating himself. There was a soft little thud as the painter dropped into the canoe. Josh lifted the paddle.

As it dipped strongly in the water and the canoe shot away from the landing, another extraordinary thing happened. Somewhere in Maggy's consciousness there was a kind of sharp white blink like lightning. It was a bright flash which seemed to illuminate actions and even words, linking them into a clear black and white pattern.

It was gone, as swiftly as it had come.

Kirk shouted, "What are you doing?" and lunged toward Josh.

The canoe rocked perilously.

Josh said, "Look out. You'll turn it over." The canoe was already beyond the shallow water, out into the deep current. "We're going out into deep water. Then I'm going to scuttle the canoe. I can swim and Maggy can swim, but you can't!"

"You can't! I'll drown—this is murder. . . ."

"Call it execution." Josh's voice was hard. The canoe shot on swiftly, too swiftly, into the swirling current. Already the landing and the line of willows were clothed in fog and seemed far away.

"I tell you, you can't do this," Kirk said in a strangled way.

"There's just one way you can save yourself," Josh said. "Tell the truth about Ralph's murder and Lydia's murder. Then I'll bring you back to land."

SEVENTEEN

The water seemed so near, so close around the little canoe. The fog closed down as if they were on a kind of island, except it wasn't an island; it was a barely visible, but dangerous, patch of water.

Kirk hunched forward. "This is absurd. You don't mean it. You hate me, you're trying to scare me. . . ."

Something flashed up in one of Josh's hands. The canoe, left to its own course, wavered and rocked. There was a thin, rending crash, and then another.

"Why, you've got a hand ax," Kirk said in a still, queer voice.

"That's right," Josh said. "And there's one air compartment gone. Next time I'll drive the ax right straight through the canoe."

The canoe had instantly lost something of its buoyancy. Maggy's seat rose a little higher. She could see Josh now, over Kirk's shoulders, and he was putting the small hand ax down beside him, out of Kirk's reach. That was the tool, then, that he had brought from the garage.

"But you can't!" Kirk said again, incredulously. "Why, even if you did scuttle the canoe, the police would know it. You can't get away with this."

"Once you're overboard, nobody will ever know what happened. I'll knock in the other air compartment, the

190

canoe will sink, it'll never be found. Maggy and I can get to shore. You can't."

"That's murder. . . ."

"It'll be an accident. The way Ralph was drowned. The way Lydia died. Another accident."

Kirk lurched forward toward Josh and the canoe lurched, too. Water splashed coldly over Maggy's knees. It struck Kirk, too, and he was afraid of water. He shrank back and then suddenly turned toward the fog-shrouded shoreline. He was going to shout for help.

Josh said, "By the time anybody hears you it'll be too late. In this fog nobody can see what I'll do. There's no boat, nothing, no way to get at you. . . . Why did you kill Ralph?"

"I didn't—I didn't—it was an accident."

"Why did you kill Lydia?"

"I didn't, I tell you. You can't . . ."

"Kirk, you don't seem to believe me. I mean it. It's perfectly safe for me. Maggy will get out, and I'll get out. But you'll drown, and nobody will ever know how it happened."

The canoe rocked. Maggy saw the flash of the hand ax. In the fraction of a second before it fell Kirk shouted, "*Don't!* I'll tell you—I didn't mean to kill Ralph. I did snatch that orange cushion, that life preserver from him. He got it first. But then I got hold of the canoe. I didn't mean to kill Ralph."

"But you did mean to kill Lydia. Why? Did she threaten you?"

"Threaten . . . ?"

"Kirk, you realize that George will find out everything there is to find out. He's suspicious now. He'll not stop until he's got at the truth. You were the cause of Lydia's divorce, weren't you? As soon as George gets onto that—and he will—he'll turn against you. He'll tell everything he knows about the works. He'll turn state's evidence in a murder trial."

"You did that. You used him against me. . . ."

"It's the truth, isn't it? Oh, you were probably too cagy to bind yourself, write any letters, anything like that. Of course, you must have made quite a play for Lydia, a conventional woman like that. She got back here and discovered that while she was getting a divorce and intending to marry you you'd got another woman—and she had some hold over you. It's the business, isn't it, Kirk? George knows all about whatever it is you're trying to do. Did he tell Lydia? Did she threaten you with that?"

"There's nothing to threaten me with."

"Oh, I think there is. I'm not sure just where and how. There are several things that you might be trying to do. There's the matter of inventory, for instance."

"We had accountants. They checked everything."

"Yes, well, how about that very successful new line of yours, small-tool kits? Weren't the boxes already sealed up for shipment when they were checked?"

"Why, probably, some of them. There was an exact check, though. Every package was rolled in on dollies and checked and then . . ."

Josh said, "Rolled back out again, I suppose, and hurriedly reloaded with more sealed boxes and counted. What was in them really? Scrap iron? Junk? It doesn't matter. That's only one trick. There must have been others, all of them adding up to a very impressive sum of assets. Did they check your accounts receivable?"

"I tell you, they looked at all our books."

"Oh well, that's only one way, another trick. Other people have tried it. It will all come out."

"But I—I don't admit any of this for a moment—but even if I had planned any sort of—of fraud, I'm not liable, now. The new stock issue has not been sold. I've not done anything illegal. You can't touch me. . . ."

"Oh, Kirk," Josh said in a curiously sad voice. "Don't give me that. This isn't the first time you've tried to cheat the stockholders. You've done it before and succeeded. A man doesn't turn into a crook overnight. It'll all come out now. And your escape hatch isn't quite ready yet."

"Escape . . . ?"

"Switzerland, wasn't it to be? Miss Emily living there, in her own house, a resident. Whenever you were ready to pull out yourself with as much of the Company's assets as you could—or if the stockholders complained of the stocks' earnings, or if anything at all went wrong—whenever you were ready to get away with all the money you could get your hands on, how simple it was going to be for you. Send money to Miss Emily. Get it deposited in a privately owned Swiss bank. No name to identify you, only a number, and you'd get away with it. That was really your aim. You didn't intend to build up the works. You intended to exploit it and get your hands somehow, anyhow, on other people's money."

"Cousin Emily! You're wrong there, you've got to admit. She wouldn't . . ."

"She wouldn't have known," Josh said somberly. "She'd have done anything you told her to do. You were looking far ahead. But Lydia threatened to stop it all, so Lydia died. And Ralph died . . ."

"Why should I kill Ralph?"

"I don't think you meant to, really. I think you figured

193

Lydia would drown in this current but Ralph wouldn't. I could be wrong."

"But—why, I couldn't manipulate an accident. I'd drown myself. . . ."

"You would drown now," Josh said. "The canoe won't float by the time I get through with it. But yesterday that was simple. All you had to do was snatch for that little life preserver, get to the canoe, hook your fingers around the keel and hold on. It wasn't much of a chance for you to take because you knew what you were going to do. You were prepared. Ralph wasn't."

"You don't have a scrap of evidence, nothing . . ."

"But I'm going to have." Josh looked around them. They were out now in the very middle of the current. "This is the place. Nobody can see or hear. Now then—jump when I tell you to, Maggy. I'll get you out." He lowered the paddle.

The canoe swirled in the strong current, tipped, and water came splashing in.

Kirk dropped down, hugging the canoe. "I'll tell you anything! Anything you want to know. Hurry, Josh—the canoe's going over. . . ."

It didn't. Josh righted it, paddling madly against the current. He said then, "You killed Ralph?"

"I got the life preserver from him. That's all. I didn't mean to kill him."

"You killed Lydia?"

"Yes—yes—anything you say."

"You tried to kill Maggy last night."

"No . . ."

"Don't try to lie. You were at the arbor. You must have followed her from the house. You heard me say that there was no case of murder without her. You were scared.

194

You lost your head. The river was near—you found a rock —but then you couldn't find Maggy. It gave you a chance to think, make some new plans. What were your new plans, Kirk? Were you going to marry Maggy and take her out of the country, and if she insisted in saying that Lydia was murdered, if she was stubborn—and she is stubborn— would there have been another accident? Sad, tragic, on her honeymoon—but no questions asked. Weren't you afraid that tomorrow would be too late?"

Yes, Maggy thought, yes—he was afraid tomorrow would be too late.

Josh said, "Was it a hard decision to make? The girl you want or your own life?"

Maggy, in her mind, replied: not very hard, really; he said good-bye to me as if he were going on a journey; he said he could do anything he had to do. And from that moment on, I became nothing to him—invisible.

"*Answer me!*" Josh said.

"All right, all right! I admit it. Anything you say. Now are we going back to land?"

Josh said slowly, "What are you planning now, Kirk?"

"Why, I . . ." For a second Maggy thought that Kirk was going to give Josh one of those flashing, apparently candid smiles; it was in his voice. But he said, "What are *you* going to do, Josh?"

There was a long silence except for the river whispering against the canoe, and the thrust of the paddle. Then Josh said, "Go back to land."

A subtle knowledge flashed through Maggy: Kirk had won, or he was going to win.

But that wasn't possible. He had confessed to murder. Josh would go to the police with the whole story. They would charge Kirk with murder. Surely Kirk knew that and had accepted it. But he hadn't accepted it, and he was going to win.

Josh was working the paddle now, hard, edging back toward the willows, which already were showing a dim silvery green line. The black roof of the house emerged from the fog above the treetops.

They approached the shallow water and Kirk said, "You can't do a thing! You forced me to say all this by threats of murder. Maggy heard it all. She'll have to tell the police that you threatened to murder me. So you see . . ." There was a faint small chuckle in his voice. "I wasn't safe before. Maggy was a danger to me. But you've canceled that—you've removed all danger from either of you because you threatened me. To save my life, I had to say anything you wanted me to say."

"They'll investigate," Josh said. "You can't stand investigation."

"Oh, but they'll investigate George! He admitted he had been to Lydia's room. The police will investigate the injured husband—the recently divorced husband, drunk and in Lydia's room just before she was found dead. If anybody is ever arrested or charged with murder, it'll be George."

"What about the fraud at the works?"

"Oh, I can fix that—do something—I'll fix that all right."

"You really think you can murder two people and get away with it, don't you, Kirk?" Josh said in a thoughtful voice.

"I know this! Even if you got me haled into court on a murder charge, no jury in the world would believe this—this so-called confession you forced me to make in order to save my life."

Josh said slowly, "But you see, Kirk, I was afraid tomorrow would be too late, too. Too late to save Maggy's life. So I had to prove it to her. The only jury I care about is Maggy. She is a jury of one."

Kirk's head jerked up. "Who's that," he said sharply, "on the landing?"

The weather-beaten landing stretched out over the water toward them. Three men stood watching them.

Two of the men were state policemen. The third, older man wore a business suit. The canoe bumped gently against the landing. One of the state policemen bent to secure the painter as Josh tossed it up to him. The older man said to Kirk, "Ralph Hewitt's body has been found. I am taking you in charge, Mr. Beall."

There was a silence. Then Kirk whispered, "But that was an accident. Really an accident. You can't charge me with murder."

"No," the older man said, "but the District Attorney can. Now, just come along quietly."

EIGHTEEN

It was all very quiet. The landing rattled a little; then the three men, with Kirk between them, disappeared around the curve of the path beside the tennis court. The roses seemed to lean down to watch.

Josh said then, in a flat, tired way, "Stay here, Maggy. Don't come to the house. I'll be back." The planks of the landing rattled lightly again and Josh was gone, too.

There was some water in the canoe, seeping through her slippers. She put her feet on the seat ahead of her. Her blue cotton dress was wrinkled and had damp patches on it, too. There was no sound at all from the house, no commotion, no shouts, nothing.

The small hand ax lay in the bottom of the canoe, its red handle in water. It seemed strange that it was merely a commonplace household tool.

She ran her finger along the rim of the canoe, which felt cold and damp.

Time passed; she knew that, and that it was important time, for it marked moments which could never be erased and never be changed. A yellow butterfly settled on the rim of the canoe and waved its wings as if debating what to do next.

But she had not debated within herself ever. She had been so sure that she was right. Face values had been convincing, yes, but mainly she had deceived herself, building up a glittering figure which did not exist. Blind, self-deluded. When had she stopped loving Kirk? And then, with another white flash like lightning, she thought, did I ever really love him?

Clare came at last along the path. Her yellow dress was the same color as the butterfly. Her face was a pale wedge between her masses of black hair. She came to the canoe. "Maggy, I want you to believe me. Last winter I thought that there was something between Kirk and Lydia. I wasn't sure—small things. But I thought so. Then when Lydia—died like that—I didn't know. I tried to warn you—I knew that there were times when Kirk would do anything in a rage—anything. But I wasn't sure—and I did want you to marry him and . . ."

"I know. . . . Don't, Clare."

"No, you must listen. I knew it was wrong to let you marry Kirk. I think I was sure in my heart from the very first, that Lydia was murdered. But then—I was afraid it was Alroy and . . ."

Maggy stepped up onto the landing and put her arms around Clare. Clare bowed her head for a second against Maggy's shoulder. Then she lifted it. "I'm all right. They want you at the house."

The house was strangely still, though, when they entered it. There was no one in the living room, no one in the hall. But in the library there were three state policemen and Josh. Clare left her at the library door. Josh said, "Sit down, Maggy, here."

She sat in the armchair before the big desk. One of the state policemen took his stand before the door. The other two stood on either side of the desk as if guarding it or something on it.

199

One of them said, "Owing to the circumstances—but this is an exception, you know. . . ."

The other policeman was busy about a tape recorder now standing on Kirk's desk. A spool of thin brown tape was already in place. The policemen were not guarding the desk; they were guarding the spool of thin brown tape. The policeman flicked a switch. He said, "This was in Ralph Hewitt's pocket when his body was found, wedged into a cove just below Berry Point. We thought it might be important. We phoned the research department of a company that manufactures these tapes. They said a tape can be immersed in water for as long as forty-eight hours and still—at least parts of it—will come out clear on the machine. They told us how to run it very slowly at first, dry it . . ."

"It's beginning," the other policeman said. "What you are about to hear is a conversation which seems to have taken place in Lydia Clowe's house."

The tape was running across from one spool to the other. It looked very small, simply a shiny brown thread, but a jumble of sound was beginning to come out of the machine into the room. There was nothing clear, only a mumble, sometimes a syllable, part of a word seemed to emerge, the high, thin timbre of a woman's voice. Suddenly then, shockingly clear, Lydia's voice said, ". . . gone only four months. Couldn't you have waited?"

Kirk's voice said as clearly, "You agreed that we mustn't write, mustn't communicate. I'd have stopped you if you had tried."

"You promised to marry me."

"Suppose I did. I've changed my mind, that's all."

"I'll not let you marry that girl. I'll stop it if I have to stand up in church and . . ."

Kirk's voice broke in, ". . . say what? You've got no proof, no letters, nothing. Don't be stupid, Lydia. I came here tonight because you asked me to . . ."

Tonight? Maggy thought—and remembered the sound of a car returning very late; she had thought it was Alroy and Clare.

Something of Kirk's magnetic charm came into the voice from the machine. "I want us to be friends. Bygones are bygones. . . ."

"If you marry that girl, I'll tell everything I know. I can ruin you, and I will. George has told me all about what you've already done and what you're trying to do at the works. You've cheated, you've stolen from the stockholders . . ."

There was a jumbled rush of sounds from the machine, a half-choked scream which was then fully choked. Something clattered as if a chair had gone over. Then with horrible clarity Lydia's voice gasped, "You—tried to—kill me. . . ."

"I *will* kill you," Kirk said with utter cold deliberation. "If you say a word to anybody, if you try to stop me, I *will* kill you."

Lydia's voice said scornfully, "How?"

"The safest way is accident." There was a sound like footsteps. A door closed hard and unmistakably.

Maggy must have made some move, for one of the policemen said sharply, "Wait. There's more. . . ."

They heard a door fling open; there were footsteps and unexpectedly a thin, frightened voice spoke, a man's voice —Ralph Hewitt's voice. "I heard everything from the next room. My tape recorder there has got it all. But we can't go through with this, Lydia. Kirk means it. He'll kill you and he'll kill me, too.

"I've got what I wanted," Lydia said. "He admitted that he promised marriage. It's on the tape recorder you brought here."

Two ghosts were talking without hindrance, freely and dreadfully.

Ralph said, "He nearly killed you just then."

"Since you were in the next room, why didn't you come to help me?"

Ralph shouted with surprising violence, "Because I was afraid! I'll have no more to do with this. It's nothing short of blackmail!"

"It's no different than it was when I talked to you today as soon as I heard about this marriage."

"You consulted me as a lawyer about a breach of promise suit."

"And you said I must have some evidence. *You* said to get Kirk here. *You* brought your tape recorder and set it up in the next room and told me to hide the microphone in this room and get some admission from Kirk, something I could use. . . ."

"I said something which would be evidence of your claims. I didn't say blackmail."

"Ralph," Lydia said softly. "I told you there'd be money in it for you. Call it blackmail or whatever you want to, *you* knew what I meant to do. Now you're scared because you heard Kirk threaten me. But you need money just as much now as you did this morning. *Don't you?*"

There was a little silence. Then Lydia said briskly, as if she had beaten down Ralph's resistance, "Tomorrow we'll both see Kirk just as I planned, tell him we've got this tape —where are you going?"

"To turn off my tape recorder . . ."

There were footsteps again, then a soft tap.

"He turned it off then," one of the policemen said. "That's all. Intent to murder. Motive. Attempted murder." He glanced at Maggy. "Ralph Hewitt had a bad head injury. Maybe a rock. Could have been made by Beall's canoe paddle. We'll never know that. But here's a motive for murder. . . . Whether the court will accept it or not —well, that's not my problem, but Beall will have a hard time getting out of this!"

He bent over the tape and turned a switch which made it run faster. The spool emptied itself swiftly on the receiving spool. Maggy watched, fixing her mind on small things —the way the policeman removed the spool, clipped a rubber band around it, the way he slid it into the inside pocket of his tunic and buttoned the tunic over it. All three of the state policemen seemed subtly relieved, and eager now to leave.

The telephone rang. Josh reached for it, but one of the state policemen took it up. "Probably for me . . ." he said, and listened. A curiously blank and uncommunicative look came into his face. "Right—yes, I understand. Yes, sir, right away."

He put down the telephone. He must have given some signal to the other two policemen, for they went out of the library all together. Josh followed them out and closed the door.

There were voices, low, in the hall, the sound receding toward the front door. After a time a car started up somewhere and another car followed it. Those sounds diminished, too. The fog outside the windows was darkening in the early twilight.

The door opened and Mrs. Elwell came in. She had Maggy's dark blue silk coat. She put it around Maggy's shoulders. "I'll take care of Miss Emily. I promise you."

She was very pale. She thrust the big handbag the nurses had given Maggy into her hand. It felt heavy, which vaguely puzzled Maggy. "I think everything you'll need is here. Now I'll see to things here. He's waiting for you."

Josh was in the hall. Clare's car was standing at the front door. Josh put her into it and went around to get behind the wheel. Probably, she thought vaguely, he was taking her to police headquarters, the police barracks somewhere. They would question her. She was a witness. He backed the car around and as he turned down the driveway she caught a glimpse of the house. There were a few lights in the windows. Its solid walls stood unmoved, untouched, as if they would stand forever.

The gravel whispered below the tires. As they turned between stone walls and the banks of shrubbery out onto the road, she said, "Where are we going?"

"I'm taking you to your mother."

"*What?*"

"We both have passports. Your passport is in your handbag. I looked. Luckily I have one which is still valid. I made plane reservations this morning."

"But you couldn't have known . . ."

"I had to get you out of it somehow today. Before it was too late. I had to prove it to you. . . . I'd better tell you now, Maggy. There'll be no murder trial. That's what that phone call was about. Kirk wasn't handcuffed; he was only held for questioning but he knew it was the end. He couldn't face it. At Berry Point Bridge he had his chance. He couldn't swim. It was over quickly. . . . It *is* better this way, for Miss Emily and for him and—it's better. . . . It's late. We'll have to hurry."

The car shot ahead into the foggy twilight.

Yes, she thought after a long time, far better. She closed

her eyes. She couldn't see Kirk's face at all; she couldn't conjure up any image whatever. It was as if he had existed only in her imagination, as if he had never been real.

It was a long ride but it seemed a short one, for the things to think about were real; the lights of the cars they met, the beat of the engine, Josh's hands on the wheel. He parked the car and left the key at the airlines desk when he picked up the tickets. The plane was being called: Paris— Rome . . ."

They went out the gate, hurrying among other late passengers. The plane was waiting, lighted, ahead of them. Halfway across the pavement toward the plane Josh stopped. He turned her to face him. "There's something I've got to know, Maggy. Would you have married him tomorrow?"

Someone pushed past her, bumped her with a canvas airlines bag, and said, "Oh, I'm so sorry."

Josh waited, his eyes intent. She had to tell the truth. "Yes," she said. "And I'd have been sorry for the rest of my life."

"That might not have been very long. I was afraid— I had to do it this way."

"Yes—yes. Let's hurry, Josh."

Josh's eyes lighted. He gave a little laugh which seemed to share everything she knew of herself. "Oh, Maggy, I know you so well—and love you so much."

They ran together across the gleaming pavement to the lighted plane and toward something else, something as strong as the sea and the stars of their course, so it was content to await its destiny.

MIGNON G. EBERHART began to write in her early teens, "mainly," she says, "because I preferred writing to studying Caesar's *Commentaries* and algebra. There was one halcyon period during which I traded work on English themes for the solution of geometry problems, with an obliging class-mate, but, perhaps for the best, this was very brief. There was a long novel to which I could add chapters at will, and numerous plays, all of which were advisedly destroyed. In my early twenties I gathered up courage and postage stamps and sent a book-length typescript to an editor. It was ac-cepted. The story was a murder mystery and that started me on a hard but rewarding writing path. The writer hopes that a mystery novel is entertaining to read, but it is not easy to write."

Mrs. Eberhart's husband is a civil engineer, and owing to the demands of his profession, she has spent much of her life in travel and in buying, settling and then selling houses in order to move to some other city to start the process all over again. During the pauses she has written thirty-four books, many of which have been serialized in the *Ladies' Home Journal*, the *Saturday Evening Post, Collier's, Woman's Home Companion* and other magazines. She also has published numerous short stories, and there is always an incomplete play script somewhere on her desk. Some of the books and stories have been made into motion pictures and some of them dramatized for radio and television. Her books have been translated into twelve languages.